Lost Woman Within

JH Lewis

For Wouzels, Moutroe, Mongo, and Bones.

About the Author

Jh Lewis lives in Cheshire with her husband, four children and two dogs.

After a life in sales, Jh Lewis re discovered her love of writing and storytelling aged 34, and has since gone on to release her debut novel, Alluvia in early 2016.

Lost Woman Within is Jh Lewis's second novel. The follow up to Alluvia is due Mid 2017.

You can find Alluvia on Amazon, Kindle and iBooks now.

Chapter 1

From the moment the imposing electric gate closed behind her, Sarah knew this was not her life. The approach to the house was no less disorientating. Spotlights softly lit the winding drive, along which stood a few oak trees, sure and steady. She felt numb. The large white house emerged in all of its modern glory, lights spilling up the facade, reflected by the floor to roof wall of glass that appeared to be an entrance. Inside was in complete darkness.

"The children are with my parents" John offered registering her apprehension. After seventeen years of marriage he knew well enough how to read his wife. She didn't outwardly respond although inside the relief washed over her. He pulled the car to a stop. The garage door instinctively jerking into action, rhythmically opening ready to swallow her into an unknown world. Her breathing came quickly but shallow, she was unable to inhale enough air, her clammy palms tugging at the neck of her jumper.

"Sarah, honey, are you ok?"

He leaned across to touch her, his worry illuminated by the emerging light. She recoiled. Her head pressed firmly against the glass of the window.

"Stop!" she yelped "I need to get out."

A few tugs of the door and it gave way tumbling her out onto the dark tarmac and into the fresh night air. She took a long, deep breath. She took a few. Who was she? John had immediately climbed out after her the concern etched across his face.

"Please Sarah, what can I do?"

"I, I don't know. Take me home."

"We are home darling."

"NO! My home, take me to my home!"

"OK, ok, you tell me where to go and I'll take you, now, straight away, whatever you need."

"It's, its, argh" she scrunched her hands up to her eyes as she let out a frustrated scream.

"What? Tell me?" He moved cautiously towards her.

"I can't remember, oh God why can't I remember?" she leaned heavily against the big black car her fists still clenched to her forehead.

"Dr Maxwell said you would be confused, it's normal..."

"It's not normal" she snapped, looking at the imposing man in front of her, Sarah tilted her head as the realisation hit her "God. I don't even know your name."

Her tears came freely. Gently he approached her, tentatively placing a comforting arm around her shaking shoulders. With her head buried in her hands, she didn't flinch from him. Progress he dared to think for a second.

"It's ok, shhhhh its ok .John. My name is John, I'm your husband and I'm going to look after you ok? I promise. Now come on let's get you inside."

The room was in darkness, until John dropped the bags behind her and pressed a pad on the wall causing the huge room to break into a soft golden light. She stops and gasps. The vast kitchen in front of her is a world away from the misty and vague memory of her small apartment. The island in the middle takes up more floor space alone. "Welcome home!"
The tension in her shoulders is noticeable and she shifts on her feet.
"Sorry" he clears his throat "That was unthoughtful. Let me get you a drink, tea?"
Distractedly filling the large stainless steel kettle from an even larger tap it comes on too strong causing water to splash all over the light marble worktop. "Shit" he curses wiping the water from his pristine shirt. It looks expensive. It all looks expensive. She watches this man, her supposed husband, blankly as he rummages through the drawers, suddenly aware her jaw still hangs open. "Where are they?" He looks at her
Her heart quickens, does he expect an answer?
John produces a folded fluffy towel from the bottom drawer; it has small squares of navy across it that match perfectly the cupboards encircling them. "Found them, I will have to remember that! The kitchen has always been more of your domain" he smiles warmly. It's the first comforting thing she has witnessed all day.
"I will take your bags upstairs."
"John?" He turns at the sound of his name on her lips "Is there a spare room?" her cheeks redden.
"Oh of course, yes. I will put your things in there. And then I will make your drink ok?"
"Thanks" she mutters.
"Please Sarah, sit. Try to relax. You are home now. You are safe." He smiles, sighs and heads out of the room. Her body is frozen, numb even. She listens for his footsteps on the stairs only then Sarah takes the opportunity to look around what they tell her is *her* home, trying to find something, anything, familiar. The marble top is cold as she drags her fingers across it. Moving around the island she heaves open one of the two large doors by its full length brushed steel handle. White light causes her to blink. The fridge is fully and expertly stocked, everything neat and facing the right way, all the different drinks lined up. She pushes it shut. There are some letters laid on the corner of the large square dining table over by the long wall of glass. Sarah pads quietly over to them, her ear turned slightly to the hallway in anticipation of his return. She picks up the pile; they are mostly addressed to John. School trips, household bills, an official looking one with a small stamp reading Osmotica in the corner. She sifts through them all. Until she spots a credit card statement,

catching the name Sarah Ryan on the top. Curiosity forces her to quietly slip out the paper and unfold it. £14483.16 was the last statement. Beauty salons, Selfridges, Goldsmiths, the list goes on, *that's more than I earn in months* she thinks. She quickly folds it back up and replaces it carefully keeping watch for John returning. Squinting through the glass the garden is illuminated by more spotlights, revealing the large terrace leading to the perfectly manicured lawn in the distance and the fountain that holds pride of place. *Very grand.* Wouldn't she remember this? Wouldn't this be a better life for her?

"Sorry I wanted to put things away for you". His voice makes her jump, it jolts her back into this room, this life. "Let me get you that drink."

The shrill of a mobile cuts through the silence. He grabs it from the pocket of his suit trouser, his brow furrows as he swipes the front of the screen and turns slightly away from his startled wife. He lowers his voice.

"Eric! Yes. She's fine, yes, back home. No. Maybe tomorrow. I know. I will. Hey love you. Goodnight" and he clicks off.

"That was Eric. Our son." He taps the phone in his hand "He was worried."

"Oh, erm. Right, is he...?"

"Yes fine, he's fine. I think he just wants to speak to you, but don't worry I told him not yet". The momentary panic which instantly strangled her stomach releases. Before John busies himself making her drink he looks at this dishevelled woman before him, who looks exactly like his wife, sounds exactly like his wife and wonders, will he ever get her back or worse still, will she ever remember.

Chapter 2

His alarm sounds as always at 5:45am but this morning John doesn't rush out of bed, the weight of sleeplessness overtakes his usual desire to conquer the day. There is a vast void next to him, the pillows perfectly plumped, free of the indentation of her. He had faced many problems, issues, difficulties, many he was glad his wife couldn't remember, but never had he felt overwhelmed. It was an uncomfortable new feeling. He thought back to the last few days.

Dr Maxwell had waited patiently for him to finish his strained phone call before politely ushering him into a private room and closing the door behind them. Neither man had waited to sit before they spoke "Is she awake?"

"Not yet, but it won't be long. She has been heavily sedated and will wake up confused."

"But everything is good?"

"Yes, everything is good" the doctor had reassured him.

He hoped it was. Walking into that room had been more difficult than even he, John Ryan, CEO for god sake, had anticipated. The man who controlled everything, even down to the cut of his Saville Row suits, had felt something alien to him. Nervous.

Today though, today he would unwittingly grant himself a lie in which allowed Sarah to rise first even though she woke well after ten. She had hardly slept. Even when the mattress had moulded around her aching body, the crinkly plush duvet had engulfed her, and she immersed herself in the huge soft pillows, sleep would not come. Lying there, she too thought back. How the beeping and the quiet hum of machines had woke her gently from a deep sleep. What she would give for that sleep now. Her head had hurt, a lot, it was the first conscious thought in her mind. The second was where was she? Her eyes had strained against the light as the hospital room had come into focus, and she had to lift her aching arm up to protect herself from the glare. A figure appeared in the room. His name tag had read Dr Edward Maxwell. He made no attempt to speak, merely picked up his chart and assessed the machines. His head nodded, which could only have been a good thing, although she hadn't the energy to ask. That's when the door had opened a second time and he entered. Tall, and well built, wearing a suit. Definitely not medical staff she thought, a lawyer maybe?

"Sarah? Sarah can you hear me?" he had spoken his first words to her.

"I'm just checking her over" The doctor had informed him.

She'd felt the cold metal sting against her chest and had, once again, been blinded by searing light flashing in her eyes.

"Sarah, my name is Dr Maxwell, do you know where you are?" he'd clicked away his torch and returned it to his top pocket. She'd watched this process through foggy eyes. She managed one feeble disorientated nod. Yes she had known where she was but what she did not know was why.

"Do you know why you are here?" The doctor asked, she remembered the sliding glance to the lawyer, understanding now what that had involved even though neither had offered an explanation at that point. Her eyes met the lawyers. She remembered his arms folding firmly across his chest showcasing his muscles through the tightness of his shirt. She remembered clearly her panic, as she suddenly became alarmed there could be damage to her. Subconsciously and frantically she checked her body, her head, her shoulders, her brain running down her torso and over her legs. She clenched her fists, wiggled her toes, but there had been no pain, just the dull ache of an anaesthetic.

"You had an accident, nothing to worry yourself about but we would like to keep you in for observation for a few days" the doctor finally offered.

"No! That's not what we agreed she is coming home with me."

Why would the lawyer say that she had thought? Who would defy a doctor?

"I don't advise that Mr Ryan" the doctor had argued through gritted teeth but he hadn't got his way. She would go home with the lawyer, but not before she had violently vomited. She had dutifully dressed, although dazed and unsure, with the help of some nurses. As she was being led out of the room the doctor had made a last minute grab of her wrist "Sarah, do you have any questions?" he looked intently into her eyes. She thought she could see sadness, but dazed her mind raced. Questions, yes, she had about a million but the only one she could gather the strength to utter was "Why do you keep calling me Sarah?"

How long could she stay here, cocooned in such sanctuary this quiet bedroom afforded her? Natures call forced her to concede and after avoiding the mirror in the bathroom, she slipped on the robe hanging from the door and cautiously ventured out.

"You scared me!" she yelped. John was mid knock when she had opened the door, he threw his hands up defensively not wanting to startle his vulnerable wife.

"Sorry!"

"It's ok" she answered pulling her dressing gown closer.

"How did you sleep?" he ventured.

"Not great."

"Me either really. But as I lay awake I had an idea, do you mind?" he gestured to sit on the bed behind her but she wasn't ready to let him into the only place that felt remotely hers. She stepped out onto the landing and shut the door.

"Over coffee?" she asked,

"Of course, of course. Anything you like."

On entering the kitchen, Sarah in Johns wake, they were greeted with humming and laughter which instantly stopped on sight of the couple.

"Marcia, Clarissa, can you leave us please? And you Bill."

The two ladies nod and with a wide eyed glance at Sarah they scuttle out of the room.

"Breakfast is made sir. I will await instructions for the day." Bill answers, before smiling kindly past John to Sarah and following his colleagues out.

"Who are they?" Sarah asks quietly.

"Oh, Marcia and Clarissa are our housekeepers and Bill is the family chef. Sit I will make coffee. Do you want breakfast? He's an excellent cook." John opens the silver serving trays on the kitchen top.

"We have eggs, sausage, bacon, toast, avocados, tomatoes, and omelette?" Sarah's stomach grumbles in response but the nausea of being here eliminates any possibility of eating. She shakes her head "Just coffee please. Housekeepers? Chefs?" she mutters

"Yes darling" John lets out a little chuckle "I always try to provide what you need."

"Oh, thanks" she answered, but unsure as to why.

With steam rising from the fresh cups John pulled in the chair next to her, at the same dining table she had walked around last night, careful to keep a bit of distant between them. The sun was high in the blue sky outside, the light dancing across the cascading water in the distant fountain. Turns out it was a mermaid standing proud in the middle, she could now see in the daylight.

"Shall I open the doors? Let in some fresh air?" John offered, following his wife's gaze.

"Hmmm. Oh, yes. Please would you mind?"

"No, not at all."

He rose with ease, with athletic grace, punched in some numbers on a screen by the door and immediately the glass started to retract, allowing the huge kitchen to become a part of the terrace. The sounds of a busy autumnal day bled in, the birds singing, the breeze rustling through the trees. The air smelt fresh and sweet, like newly cleaned laundry.

"We could sit outside in the sun if you like?" John gestured to the cream sofas adorning the terrace, but she shook her head, feeling far to disorientated to leave the safety of this house just yet, even to the terrace. John resumed his place next to her and produces his phone from his jeans pocket.

"Some pictures."

He unlocks it with a number that's familiar to Sarah but she cannot recall why, suddenly her smiling bronzed face fills the screen she makes a small gasping sound.

"In Malta last year" he points to her image "we have a villa there, you love it."

She stares blankly at the screen, her palms, folded neatly in her lap, begin to sweat. He clicks on the photo app and once again her face fills the screen only this time she is wrapped in the arms of the man before her and they are smiling.

"Macy took this, our daughter."

Sarah glances up at him but quickly turns back wide eyed as he continues to scroll through. She sees picture after picture of them together, on the beach, his arms around her in a kitchen, him kissing her in a restaurant, and then two teenagers appear.

"See, there she is, with her brother, our son Eric." he searches her face. Sarah's eyes prickle with tears, blurring out the rest of the happy picture leaving only the boy's beaming face in sharp focus. Her heart pounds. John instinctively reaches across to embrace her but she pulls away.

"Get off me!" her hands fly to her face, rubbing at her eyes to clear away the tears

"Sorry! I'm sorry" he says leaning back,

"Please it's too much I can't." Sarah stutters now, starting to sob into her hands.

The children are beautiful there is no doubt of that, the girl has her father's blonde hair and hazel eyes, her skin slightly pink from the sun , but the boy he is darker, tanned much deeper than his sister, and his silky brown eyes resemble Sarah's memory of her own. How can this be? John slowly places his hand on her convulsing shoulder but Sarah doesn't have the energy to push him away again.

"No. No you're wrong. I don't believe you" she cried after seeing her life, a life she had no recollection of. A lie. How can she have given birth to two children and not know it? She must have scars, hints of a pregnancy, of a birth? She wanted to frantically search herself, to see if her body betrayed her mind. How could she have experienced the supposedly happiest day of her life and hold no memory of it. To look into the pleading eyes of the man in front of her without recognition. His words struggled to hold meaning. Drowned out by the beating of her own heart and the racing of her own blood in her ears. She was unaware of the frantic shaking of her own head in protest.

"I'm sorry, I thought it would help .You know with your memory."

Sobbing she looks directly at him,

"With my memory? I remember, but my name is not Sarah its Ava, and I don't know who any of you are"

Somewhere across town a doctor was turning in after yet another long night shift. He heaved his aching body onto the bed, the silence of his empty home comforting. Adele must have taken the boys to school. It wasn't just the work that weighed on him, there was something else, something he forced down where he almost couldn't feel it at every moment. Guilt. It was only a few days ago, but time had ticked so mercilessly he could have sworn weeks had passed. He replayed it in his mind. He had left her in the room knowing it would be sometime before she woke, the drugs he'd administered earlier made sure of that. He'd had a more pressing issue. He needed to speak with her husband. John Ryan had been easy to spot, he was taller than most and always wore a suit with the finest cut. There was more money in that one piece of tailoring than most of the people in the plush waiting room he paced wore collectively, he remembered thinking. John held his phone to his ear. Every few moments he ran his hand through his short, perfectly coiffed blonde hair. Today however, his normal air of composure was cracked. Dr Maxwell had been the Ryan family doctor for years. Long enough to witness John become CEO of his father's Sports Wear brand at a mere forty five, that, he believed, allowed John Ryan Senior to while away his days at the golf club and his wife Rita in the jewellers. That day though, John's agitation was palpable. He turned locking eyes with his doctor and marched into his office.

"I want to take my wife home now" he had demanded arms folded signifying this was a statement as opposed to a question.

"Ok if she is ready." was all he had said, was the only fight he had put up. *Pathetic.* Even after their words in Sarah's room there seemed no movement in John's resolve.

"She is ready, she will be better there than in here, prepare her" and John marched out of his office. Edward sat alone for a while, the weight of the day playing on his mind, but John Ryan is a paying client, and without admitting her, the person responsible for Sarah. There was little he could have done to stop him. So with the pen heavy in his hand Edward had signed her release papers even though his mind screamed against it.

He lay back on the bed and closed his eyes. *You should have fought harder.*

Chapter 3

"Miss Ryan can you stop that incessant tapping!"

Her head snaps up, all eyes have fallen on her and some sniggering can be heard around the theatre.

"Sorry." She mumbled. The lecturer settled back into her steady droll, Macy places down her pencil and sits back in her chair trying with all her might to focus on the monotonous tones coming from her teacher.

"What's wrong with you?" The dark haired girl sitting next to her whispered. She had known Leah since the first day of boarding school where, through their joint distress and isolation, they had found comfort.

"Nothing, I'm fine" she whispered back.

"Oh yea, you seem fine! I told you not to come back so soon"

"It's not that soon Leah I can't stay off forever."

"It's only been four weeks Mace"

"I need to concentrate on something other than mum, get back to normality... whatever that is"

"Shhhhhhh." they hear from the boy behind

"Oh fuck off Sean" Leah spat back at him

"Miss Ryan. Miss Harrow! Is there something you wish to share with the class?" They both look up, Macy reddening at the fact she has twice now been reproached in front of everyone.

"I was just asking Sean to be quiet" Leah shouted grinning. Sean booted the back of her chair, Leah flicked him the birdie under the desk in response. The exchange made Macy smile. The bell rang. Scraping of chairs, clatter of footsteps and the instant sound of chatter drowned out the teacher calling for homework.

"Come on lets grab some lunch" Leah says a few steps ahead

"Why do you have to be such a dick Leah?" Sean asks, shoulder barging Leah out of the way but slipping Macy a soft smile as he passes.

"Oh it was a joke, no need to get your knickers in a twist" she rolls her eyes at Macy. Sean turns slowly and punches Leah lightly on her arm, with his rucksack pulled securely over his shoulder he sulks off.

"Ouch, that prick. I think he likes me" she winks.

"You are messed up Leah Harrow, you are messed up." Macy laughs.

The canteen is too noisy to rest. Macy rubs at her temples trying, in vain to ease the soaring pain ripping through her head, her phone bleeps in her pocket.

Hi Honey. How is college? Mum seems ok, she just gone for a shower. Love you dad x

A shower. It seems such a normal everyday thing to do but she wonders how it must feel for her mother. A strange shower, in a strange house.

All ok. Good glad she's doing ok. Can we come home yet, I promise I won't come out of my room? x

I need my space back she thinks. Plus she can no longer bare the overpowering nature of her grandfather. The phone bleeps again.

Maybe tomorrow ok x

"No dad! That's not ok!"

She realises she shouted this out loud by the quizzical looks and sniggers thrown her way from students sitting at the tables surrounding her. She is alone. Her tray of food untouched. Her open satchel on her lap.

"Squeeze up" Leah places down her tray and notices the staring "Fuck off the lot of you, go on, there's nothing to see!" The jeering faces turn away.

"Thanks" Macy offers feebly.

"Dickheads"

"Sooo, I still can't go home"

"What? How do you know?"

Macy wiggles the phone in front of Leah's round face, she sighs, "I just want my life back! Why does this have to happen to us?"

"I dunno Mace, I mean, it's the kinda thing you read about not something that actually happens, car crash, memory loss, it's like a movie you know."

"Yea a bad movie…"

"Those movies always have a happy ending." Leah grins at her a mouth full of spaghetti.

"Do they Leah? Do they?" she throws the piece of cucumber she was nibbling on her plate and huffs as she pushes the tray away.

"Hey! Macy! Everything will be ok" Leah puts a comforting hand on her shoulder "I promise."

Staring at the second hand rhythmically jerking round the clock face made time cease to have meaning. What did she need time for anyway? Who did she need time for? It was six pm and they had managed to numbly muddle through the pointless day, one awkward moment after another. Flashes of her past intermittently assaulted her thoughts. A small glimmer of a once well-known face, the smell of a roast cooked chicken in a forgotten kitchen, the sound of a familiar laughter. It muddled her mind. Like a fog encircling her brain just occasionally breaking, allowing her a short tantalising peek. The kitchen door edged open, Sarah jumped.

"Oh, God, sorry, I was just going to sneak in"

Sarah's face dropped. She was him, but astonishingly laced with her, Sarah could see it as clear as day.

"Erm. Hi I'm Macy"

"Hi I'm Ava"

She could just spot the gathering of the girl's eyebrows, the slight tilt of her head and the glisten of water brimming at the corner of her eyes. Strangely she instinctively wanted to comfort her

"I take it you still can't remember?" Macy looked down, picking at her fingers

"Um, I'm sorry, I really am sorry"

She sighed "It's ok" but Macy was lying to protect this woman she loved

"Your dad is somewhere through there" Sarah pointed down the long corridor separating the Kitchen from the main lounge, keen to release this girl from her motherless torture. Macy knew her dad would be in his office, it was down there, along with the games room, a library and a home cinema they had installed for last Christmas but she guessed her mum didn't remember any of that.

"Oh actually mum..." they both froze at the casual use of the word, it hung awkwardly between them "Um, can I run upstairs without you telling dad I'm here?"

"Sure" she smiled.

"Great. Ok, well then" She pulled her bag closer to her "see you in a bit" and she was gone, leaving Sarah once again alone but this time with a shared secret, however small, to connect them.

It occurred to him the difference in her was she was smiling. An emotion he had not witnessed on his wife's face since before the accident over four weeks ago now. It lit up her features, lost the years from her face. Small lines fed out from the corners of her warm brown eyes. Her full lips turned upwards. She was beautiful.

"Everything ok Sarah?" John asked.

"Oh! You made me jump" she looked up from the paper she was reading "Yes ok. Thank you. I have just been thinking"

"Hmmm, thinking?"

"Yes" she twitched in her seat at the same table.

"Thinking about what honey?"

She flushed at the endearment but choose to ignore it.

"My mind is muddled, I get these memories but I just can't quite hold on to them, so I thought, maybe, I could try hypnotherapy. There are these adverts in the paper, can you help me choose one?"

She spotted the clenched cup in his hand, watching with intrigue the white appear on his knuckles. "Sure. Great idea, but maybe we should leave it a while, see if things come back to you first"

"But things are coming back to me, different things..."

"What things?" he almost demanded.

She looked away from him "Things that mean I'm not who you think I am"

"Look around you Sarah, this house, these photos, is this not proof enough that what I am telling you is the truth?"

"No! Because it's not the truth, my name is Ava Gabriel, I work in the HR department of a small firm in Manchester..."

"Just stop it!" The volume of his words made her body tense, she inhaled sharply. He realises instantly his mistake "I'm sorry, honey I'm really sorry, this is hard for me you know" he slides into the seat next to her. She doesn't respond "Please forgive me?" he smiles pleadingly.

"Where's the phone?"

"Phone? It's over there on the wall, why?"

Sarah marches over to it punching in the familiar number of her mother's only to be met with a disconnect tone. She stares at the buttons willing another number to appear in her mind, but there is only blankness. The firm. What is it called? Frustrated she hits herself with the handset on her forehead over and over.

"Sarah stop!" John rushes over "Please don't. Give that to me" he tries to prise the phone from her hand. "Get off, get off me" She grips on to it, lashing out at him "Get off! John!" she screams.

He grabs her arm ripping the handset violently out of her hand causing it to crash to the white tiles beneath her feet. Sarah stops struggling. He will always over power her. She is only slight and stands no more than 5'4, he towers above her.

Sobbing she slides down onto the floor picking up the smashed pieces and moving them out of the way he slides down next to her. "I'm sorry" she whispers.

"It's ok. I just don't want you to hurt yourself"

"I don't know who I am" she cries.

"I know honey. I know"

He places his arm around his wife in time to spot Macy rushing in to see what all the commotion was.

"You're not supposed to be here for a reason Mace" John starts after settling Sarah down to sleep. Macy is lying under her duvet staring at the ceiling.

"I know dad, but I just wanted to be home, it's been four weeks. I need my own space"

"You mean you can't cope with Grandfather anymore?" he smiles, sitting at the foot of her bed.

"Well yeah, that too! Do you think she will mind? Mum, if I stay?" she turns to her father.

"Mace, it's not mum yet, you know that right? She doesn't remember who she is, she may never remember". Macy pulls the blanket tighter around herself "Yeah I know"

He puts a reassuring hand on his daughter "One day at a time Mace ok" he gets up grabbing the remote from the wooden bedside table and passing it too her "As you're here, you may as well stay now" he grins, kissing her head.
"Thanks dad" she smiles "you're the best!" and she flicks on the large wall mounted TV.
"I'm off to get your brother, I won't be long"

Chapter 4

John Snr and Rita owned a large estate about a mile down the road on the outskirts of Cheshire. It took John less than ten minutes before he was climbing the familiar stone steps on which he had played as a child. As he placed his foot on the last stair the thick wooden door creaked open and he was greeted with his mother's discerning face "She's been here"

"Hello mother! Great to see you" he mocked "Eric here?"

He slipped inside skimming a soft kiss on her cheek as he passed.

"You can't ignore this John"

"Yes, Yes. Where is he?"

She followed behind her son, who may have towered above her in height but she made up for stature in weight. A large set lady, decorated in jewels. Hair kept short and dark, framing a full face iced with make-up. She even smelt expensive.

"The sitting room, with Horace" she pointed, the diamond on her finger cascading spots of rainbow upon the wall. Eric was on the floor, happily rolling round being licked across his face, causing fits of giggles.

"Hey Buddy"

"Dad!" Eric jumped up and embraced his father.

"Horace down" demanded John Snr as he folded the broadsheet and rose from his chair "Son" both men shook hands.

"Father"

"How's mum?" Eric's deep brown eyes looked helplessly at his father as he asked.

"She's doing great bud, honestly really great" he ruffled his hair "I'm here to take you home"

"Really?!"

"Really, now go grab your stuff"

"Yes!" he ran from the room punching the air, his father watching in amusement.

"Sit down boy, we need to talk" John Snr was not the kind of man anyone ever said no too, even his own son. John lounged back on one of the great soft blue chesterfields that dominated even this vast room. He ran his sweaty palm through his hair "To start with, how is Sarah?"

"She's struggling dad. What more can I say"

"It's an awful tragedy she has been through" Rita offered sitting down, the rattle of the ice in her gin and tonic accompanying that of her jewellery.

"What exactly does she remember Jay?"

Jay. His father had called him that for as long as he could remember. It differentiated them he had argued, but his mother remained staunch in her refusal to call him anything but his full name.

"It's as expected. She seems to be suffering from some kind of complication, she thinks she is someone else"

"Really?" his mother asked, coughing on a piece of ice.

"What did Edward say her prognosis was?" John Snr asked ignoring his wife's difficulties.

"He doesn't know dad, that's the problem"

"Hmmm we need to be cautious …And what about this other problem son? Your mother informed you of our visitor I take it?"

"Yes she did mention it, instantly."

"She can't just bloody turn up here. What are we supposed to do? What if, god forbid, the children saw? What then?" his mother exclaimed.

"Just leave it to me ok" he stood.

"You better take care of it Jay, I won't stand for it. You have your new chance here"

"Yes father"

Eric ran back in the room just in time to end all further conversation, much to John's relief. "Right all packed?"

Eric nodded enthusiastically.

"Come on son, let's go home".

Eric knew the journey would be short but he couldn't complete it without asking. He had to. The scene had disturbed him. *I'll wait for the right moment when we are close enough to home* he thought. His dad was humming, tapping the steering wheel in time to the music. Eric didn't recognise it, something with an electric guitar maybe? The car still harboured the fresh new leather scent after only being registered and delivered last month, even though it looked exactly like the last one. He wound down the window letting in some of the last dregs of summer sunshine to mask the smell. He took a deep breath.

"Dad, someone came to grandma's last weekend when I was home"

"Hmmm?"

He sensed his father shift slightly in his seat, the tapping stopped.

"There was an argument at the door, quite a bit of shouting; I went to look from the top window"

"Yes?"

"Well, there was a woman. Trying to get inside. To get to you" he looked across to his father.

"What do you mean to get to me?" his cheeks coloured.

"She wanted you"

"How do you know she wanted me Eric?" John attempted to chuckle.

"Well. She was screaming your name"

He watched the expression fall on his father's ashen face as the gate slid shut behind them. Neither uttered another word until well inside the house.

Chapter 5

The water swills, rising up slowly. Tumbling crescendos of gushing liquid, swirling. Dancing within its own vortex ballet. Steam fills the room, the whoosh of the water cascading from the taps plays in the background. She is enveloped in a fluid warmth.
His dark arms wrap around her. Her wet hair sticking to his muscular chest.
"Ava?" she hears

"Tom!"
"What did you say?" John asked startled.
The memory had shocked her. As quickly as it came, it disappeared. Only now, it had etched into her psyche. Tom. She remembered. Fleetingly. The sound of his sweet, deep voice. They were lay together, his strong, tattooed arms embracing her. Their fingers intertwining. His face though, still blurred, cloudy, but she can just see his sparkling green eyes; like sunlight across the ocean, but rest of his face, frustratingly, she cannot quite reach. This is real.
"What did you say honey?" Johns repeated question jolted her.
"Sorry?" she blinked.
"You said something? Sounded like "Tom"?" He peered over from his place at the table.
"Did I? erm…I don't know, I can't remember, daydreaming that's all" she lied.
"Look" he rose and moved towards her "Let's go out tonight, we've been stuck in this house for over a week now! There's this favourite little restaurant of ours, maybe doing something familiar will help? Just the two of us? What do you say?"
It was true, they had been prisoners in this house, John refusing even to go to the office, only leaving the house to drop Eric at boarding school last Monday and picking him up at the end of the week. Seven awkward days.
Macy had milled in and out. Mostly avoiding both her parents. Sarah dancing round Bill, Marcia and Clarissa, still awkward at the thought of having 'staff'. The only saving grace was the amount of hours John spent glued to his mobile, allowing her to explore her new surroundings. She found much of it didn't hold her interest.
"Sarah?" His voice interrupted her thoughts. Go out together? He was her husband, wasn't he? She had loved him at some point, she must have, if all this is was true.
"Erm…."
"You can get dressed up, have a root through your dressing room, pick a nice outfit. It will be a treat" he smiled broadly. Sarah contemplated his extended hand for a moment as if they were doing one of his many business deals. Calmly she took it, mentally reminding herself to breath as, for the first time,

his fingers wrapped around hers. His face erupted into a wide smile showcasing his exceptionally white teeth and those hazel eyes twinkled.

"Come on" he said as he led her up the stairs "I will show you where you keep everything"

"Ok sure" she answered.

"Hey mum?" Macy poked her head through the doorway and froze "Wow! You look amazing!"

"Erm, really?" Sarah blushed.

"Really! That dress is my favourite, the red really suits you" she hastily entered the room as Sarah stroked down the figure hugging material. "Not too, you know, tight?"

"Not at all! You look a knock out mum" her face was alight but Sarah still felt uneasy at the use of her daughter's term. She took a moment to briefly scrutinise Macys smiling face. Tall and statuesque, she had the body only supermodels were blessed with, her long blond hair tied high in a ponytail made her childlike features appear even more youthful. She was beautiful, and Sarah waited, hoping for the wave of love to consume her. "What jewellery will you wear?"

"Hmmm?"

"Jewellery?" Macy repeated.

"Jewellery? I don't know what jewellery I have?"

"Come with me!" her daughter chuckled "You will love this"

She almost dragged her to the polished dark walnut island in the middle of the room. It matched the wardrobes encasing it. Gently and carefully Macy opened the dark velvet lined drawer. Sarah gasped.

"Hahahaha see I knew you would love it"

"Wow!" Sarah breathed. She had never before seen such a glittering array of jewels. *Nothing like the small wooden, sequin lined, trinket box that flashed in her memory like a passing racing car. She bought it whilst on holiday in Thailand, it held only her gold bangle and ruby ring, the only pieces she owned with any value.*

"Dad sure knows how to treat a lady" Macy grinned, picking out diamond droplet earrings and putting them up to Sarah's ears, the memory of Thailand had gone. Slipped away again as fast as it came.

"May I?" Macy asked.

Sarah nodded, and didn't flinch at her touch as Macy expertly put in the earrings.

"Now just this....."

She slipped a diamond and ruby tennis bracelet around Sarah's bare wrist

"And of course these! These though, you will have to put on yourself"

Sarah felt something considerable drop into her hand. She stared wide eyed. In her open palm lay three rings. A simple, thin, rounded platinum band with an engraving on the inside. A huge diamond, the size of a garden pea, seated proudly, and a ring made purely of round diamonds, each one must have been at least half a carat each. She finally closed her gaping mouth and looked up at her beaming daughter "Amazing aren't they?" Macy grinned.

"These...are. Mine?" she stuttered.

"Of course! That's your wedding band, engagement ring, and eternity ring. He bought you the last one when I was born". The two women looked at each other. Their elation now tainted with sadness. Sarah's eyes started to fill.

"No! Stop, don't cry you will ruin your make up. Now look" she pushed her mother in front of the mirror "Beautiful."

Sarah smiled. For the first time in what she could remember she felt good. Her blown out brown hair lay at her shoulders, silky and smooth. Her face had colour and vibrancy, thanks mostly to eyeliner and red lipstick. She looked at her daughter through the mirror, something about her was familiar. Exceptionally familiar.

"Are you read....wow!" John stopped "Sarah. You look beautiful"

Macy smiled "Have fun you two" she kissed her dads cheek before whispering "I love you" and bouncing out of the room.

Sarah watched her go. She must spend more time with Macy, and the other one, what was his name again?

"You...You look...Wow" John stared, causing Sarah to flush and look away.

"Thank you. She had, erm, sorry I had, a good wardrobe"

"I see Macy showed you the drawer" he nodded to where it still sat open and glistening.

"Yes! Oh God! It's like Goldsmiths in there! That's an impressive collection" she laughed and the sound of it took Johns breath away.

"Well you're an impressive lady"

She felt her cheeks redden again.

"Thanks" she mumbled

"So are you ready?"

"Yes! I think so. Oh but I have these" she held out her open palm "I'm not sure what to do with them?" Recognition lifted his face and he nodded.

"Well, what would you like to do with them?" John enquired softly. She shrugged. What was the correct protocol for wedding rings to a man you didn't remember, let alone remember marrying.

"Why don't you try them on? See how they feel?" he offered. Sarah looked at him and hesitated. He picked them carefully from her, she noticed the glint of the platinum band adorning his own left hand and it sent shivers of guilt and something else she couldn't quite place down her spine. Taking all three rings at once he slipped them easily onto her forth finger.

"There. How do they feel?"

She turned her hand over, watching them sparkle and dance.

"Heavy" she grinned.

The restaurant was small and intimate with soft lighting and a hum of gentle music in the background. They were shown immediately to a velvet seated booth at the back, affording them some privacy. It appeared to Sarah that, in this life, good things came lined in velvet. The tables were draped in thick, searing white cloth and the crystal glasses created tiny fragments of light. It was quintessentially romantic she thought as the waiter filled a glass with red wine. John took a gulp and swirled it around his mouth.

"Yes, thank you" he said, the waiter pouring the glugging blood liquid into the deep crystal. Silently they each pondered the large menu in front of them. "You really do look so beautiful tonight" he offered leaning slightly closer to her.

"Please stop" she flushed.

"What?" He laughed "A man isn't allowed to tell his wife how gorgeous she is?" Sarah shifted in her seat. She allowed a moment to pass and waited for him to pick up his glass before sneaking a glance back up at him. The suit he wore was dark navy, with a waistcoat, and the light blue of his shirt accentuated his fair features. It hung unbuttoned at the neck just enough to pique her interest as to what was underneath. He was broad she noticed, once again she was drawn to the outline of his muscles as his arm moved to replace his glass. She wondered how he looked without the clothes. Then it hit her, he had seen her naked. Fully naked. In fact, if what they told her was true he had even seen her give birth, twice. To her though, he was a complete stranger and she no more knew him, than the waiter that had served them. Her heart quickened with horror. He stood oblivious to her internal panic, slipping of his jacket laying it carefully across the seat.

"Shall I take yours?" he smiled down at her.

"Erm yes, ok" Sarah gulped. As she wriggled to get out of the matching red jacket he took the top of it, his fingers brushing her shoulders and down her arms as he slipped it off her. He held her seat out, allowing her to sit back down, sliding it in behind her before resting her jacket on top of his. Sarah's whole body tingled.

"Have you decided what you would like to eat?"

It was a normal question but under the gaze of those perfect hazel eyes she couldn't manage a coherent answer.

"Erm, well, whatever. You chose" she placed the menu on the table "I mean you know me better than I do at this moment so, I trust you, to choose"

He sat back and sighed "I wish it wasn't like this"

Sarah smiled feebly, not sure what reassurances she could offer him "Ah well, I suppose I could look at this as an opportunity" he picked up the glass again this time swilling the wine before taking a long glug.

"An opportunity?"

"It's not every day you get the chance to make your wife fall in love with you all over again" he grinned, relishing the sight of her blushed cheeks. Sarah turned down her gaze and focussed on the thick stem of glass between her fingers.

"So I guess this would make this a first date?"

"I guess so! To our first date" he held up his drink and she smiled at the ding of the glasses, but inside her stomach was doing somersaults.

"Ok then, tell me John. What is it you do for a living?" she took a large sip of wine

"I, we, own a sports wear brand"

"Really? One I would know?" Sarah whispered, unsure why she did.

"Well he knows it over there, and him, oh and him. They're wearing our footwear"

Sarah spun round eager to see, only to be greeted with strange looks. They both laugh "Not very subtle Sarah!"

" Oops, no not very really. Is sportswear appropriate for this kind of establishment?" she enquired still smiling.

"The wine starts at a hundred and fifty pound a bottle, customers can wear what the hell they want in this kind of establishment" his wide smile dazzles her.

A hundred and fifty a bottle. That is more than she could ever afford before, that she knew for sure.

"Tell me then, what do you do?" he rests his elbows on the table, his large hands clasped beneath his chin, looking straight into her eyes.

"Me? Um. I...." she struggles to know what to tell him "I work in HR, I think"

"HR?! Really, for who?" his question is soft and gentle, not aimed to make her uncomfortable, and it didn't.

"I'm, not quite sure. Oh! I have an assistant Mabel, wait! I have assistant! That's the first time I have remembered that!" Johns smile sliped momentarily

"Don't you know? Where I work? Am I right?" she asks, just before John inhaled enough air to answer the waiter arrived interrupting, allowing John some time. He has some quick thinking to do.

"Can I take your order sir?"

"We will both have the usual" John answered.

"Excellent choice, the chef has some fine cuts imported from Portugal this evening...."

Great, great, blar, blar. Hurry up Sarah thought as the waiter launched into a monologue of details about the beef and its accompaniments.

"I will fill your glasses" the red liquid seemed to slow as he poured it, each monotonous churn taking longer and longer. Finally with their steaks noted on his pad, their glasses full, the waiter left.

"Please tell me about me" she begged.

"Yes, you had a job in HR but that was a long time ago honey, before Eric was born. You did have an assistant, I can't remember her name, could be Mabel. In fact, yes, I'm pretty sure it was. You didn't stay long, you became pregnant" The thought of being pregnant was so alien to her. Can she really have been through all that? Her hands instinctively went to her stomach.

"Don't worry" he reached over and touched her arm "It will come back slowly, and until then I will do as I promised, look after you" he lifted one of her hands to his lips and kissed it softly. Sarah's worries momentarily melted.

Chapter 6

"Mace it's my turn to pick a film, last weekend you made me watch The Notebook and that was boring!"

"Boring? How can you say that! It's beautiful and lovely and warm and ..."

"You cried for 24 hours straight"

She threw the cushion at her brother's head. It expertly caught him just as he was putting a handful of popcorn in his mouth, causing it to spray across the red carpeted floor, Macy burst into giggles.

"Macy! Ya idiot, now I've got to pick all that up!" he snatched the remote from her before dropping to the floor, popping the corn piece by piece into his mouth "I'm definitely picking the film now"

"Ewwww that's disgusting Eric. Really? From the floor?"

"I don't want to waste it" he mumbled finding a few rogue pieces at the back of the red velvet couch that followed the contour of the walls. He dragged one of the matching footstools by his feet so he could lay right back.

"Comfy?" Macy spied her brother.

"Yes thanks" he rested the bowl on popcorn on his chest.

"You are gross little brother!"

He stuck his tongue out at her.

"Right then, what film?" she sighed.

"Step Brothers"

"Awwwww man not again!"

"What? It's my favourite! *I didn't want the salmon I told you four times*" he quoted.

"Seriously, do we have too?" she whined.

"My turn Mace!"

"Fine, fine, Step Brothers it is, for the twentieth time"

She found it on the remote and they both, if not reluctantly in Macy's case, settled back as the face of WIll Ferrell filled the projector screen.

Closed into the cinema room neither could hear the buzz of the front gate. She had been pressing for ten minutes now, knowing she was in the right place. The gate and surrounding white wall was too high to see over let alone scale and her heels wouldn't help. She took out her phone the face illuminated against the darkness. She shivered. The numbers beeped as she shakily punched them in, clasping the piece of scribbled paper in her trembling hand. Was that cold or fear, she wasn't sure.

"Hi yes can I have the phone number for Woodland House, 48 Eagle Lane, Cheshire please?...yep....uhuh....48.....oh really ok great. Yes please text it too me"

Unbelievably less than 10 seconds later a number appeared on her phone, was it really going to be that simple? She held her finger on it until it dialled.

The phone on the wall rang interrupting their laughter.

"Wait hahahaha pause it Eric, it's my favourite part"

Macy unfolded herself off the couch twirling her foot in an attempt to regain feeling,

"Hurry up then Mace"

She picked up the receiver "Hello....hello?"

"Who is this?" the female voice demanded,

"I'm sorry, what?"

"Who is this?" the voice demanded,

"Erm, you called here. Can I help you?" She shrugged in the response to the confusion on Eric's face.

"Is Ava there?"

"What?" Macy's mouth fell open

"Ava, is she there?"

Macy was silent. Thoughts racing through her mind. "I think you have the wrong number" she finally answered.

"Wait! Please! I'm looking for Ava its important can you help me? Is this Woodland House on Eagle Lane?"

"Who are you again?"

"I'm a friend, just a friend, I need to find her"

"Yes it is, but I'm sorry I can't help you, no one called Ava lives here" Macy could hear the lady's voice calling as she replaced the phone "Weird" she said,

"Who was it?" Eric asked.

"Some woman, she knew our address"

"She knew our address? Who was it?"

"I don't know? She didn't say and I didn't recognise her voice"

"What did she want?"

"Ava"

"Ava?" Eric pulled a face,

"I know, weird right" but Macy felt unsteady, hadn't she heard her mother mention the name Ava.

"Macy, if she knew our address do you think she might be here?"

The thought hadn't occurred to her but the moment her brother said it her heart began to thump. She grabbed the remote, frantically slamming the buttons, flicking through the different external camera angles until the driveway appeared on the screen before them. They both gasped as they caught the final glimpse of the flame haired woman sliding into her car and driving away

"Macy..."

"Yes?"

"I've seen her before"

There was a chill in the air and Sarah pulled her jacket tight as she dashed from the car to the house. John was right behind her.

"Quick let's get in" he said shivering.

She had only spent a few days in this "home" but after tonight, entering was much easier. At least she thought.

"Thanks" she smiled dashing through the door he held open. She stood in the vast, full height entrance, kicking off her shoes the white ceramic tiles felt warm underfoot, in spite of their chilly appearance.

"Wow, its freezing out there! Fancy a drink to warm up?" he offered,

"Sure" she smiled,

"Great"

"John?"

"Yes?" he answered looking back at her.

"I had a good time tonight" she said,

"Me too" he smiled.

As she followed him towards the kitchen Macy appeared startling her and causing her to jump.

"Dad someone was here!" Macy panted, a figure appearing in her wake. The young boy was as tall as Sarah, his dark curls sitting messily a top his head. He had a strong structure to his face, she recognised his dark, chocolate eyes. They made her gasp. Even she could see it, it was unmistakable. The clear way in which he wholly, and completely, resembled her.

"Hi mum" he mustered a small, unsure smile, looking shyly to his father.

"Erm Sarah, honey, this is Eric....our son"

John put his arm around the boy pulling him in closer, Eric's head dropped slightly and she could see the thickness of his dark eyelashes against his cheeks. Her heart drummed. She was certain they could all see it beating through such a tight dress. Her vision blurred momentarily. Her legs felt weak. She secretly leaned against the thick, wooden banister to steady herself.

Her husband.

Her daughter.

Her son.

"Hi Eric" the words came out small, she didn't recognise her own voice. He again looked up at his dad.

"Look everyone, everything is ok. Mum is recovering slowly, and Sarah, the children know what you have been through. Don't worry, they are happy just to have you home, isn't that right?"

"Yeah" they chimed in unison.

"No pressure honey ok" John soothed reaching for her hand which she allowed him to take. She was unable to look away from the boy though. He was mesmerising.

"Dad! Did you hear me, someone was here!" Macy started.

"Who? In the house?"

"No a woman, outside, in her car. She called the house phone. It was weird"
"Woman? What woman?"
"I don't know dad!" Macy exclaimed
"I do! I know who she was" Eric added "It was the woman at grandma and Grandpas" John froze.
"Sarah" he said turning to her "This is nothing for you to worry about honey, why don't you let me sort this out and you go get changed into something comfortable .I will get us that drink in the meantime ok?"
"Erm, are you sure, I don't mind…"
"No darling honestly." He smiled warmly rubbing the top of her arm. She nodded, conceding gratefully, ascending the stairs she caught Macy mouthing "Hi" and it made her smile. She was unable, however to look back at the boy.

Chapter 7

"It may be good for you? Jog your memory?" John had said but she knew it wasn't going to be easy. They sat silently watching the world whizz by in a blur of burnt orange, deep red and dirty brown. Leaves being torn from the branch, their last futile attempt to cling on, before another blust of wind ripped them from their summer home.

"All ready for the week ahead son?" John asked

"Yeah" was all Eric mustered.

"When's the game?"

"Thursday"

"We will be there"

"Really?" asked Eric excitedly,

Sarah's heart quickened.

"Don't see why not, what do you think honey fancy going watching our boy play football for the school team?"

She felt the burn in her cheeks and wished, for the sake of the boy, at least, that they would stop betraying her.

"Erm, sure. Great"

"Thanks mum!...er...." his cheeks now mirrored hers.

"Well. Alright, let's see how mum is ok son" John offered a desperate smile.

They drove through the pillared wrought iron gates, and up the gravelly drive to the imposing Elizabethan Manor house. A gold plaque by the side of the large oak door read

Progenies Academia:

Absque Liberis Ero I Pereo

"Ok son, have a good week and we will see you Thursday"

Eric leaned forward and kissed his dad, habitually turning to face Sarah. Before he could come closer she held out her hand to shake. After a moment he took it and muttered disappointingly "Bye mum" before climbing out. She watched him stride confidently towards the door. He was tall for his age, taller than her. Tall like his father. His hair though, the deep brown curls, that was all Sarah. Could he really be her son? He turned only once to wave and again, faced with him, all she could see was herself.

"I won't be long" John said "Have you got your mobile?"

Sarah fumbled around inside an oversized bag Macy had giving her this morning, claiming to be hers. Her fingers felt the coldness of the glass screen and pulled it out.

"Check" she smiled.

"Great, I won't be too long, your coffee will be here in a moment" John hesitated, turning to look back "Are you sure you will be ok?"

"What harm can come to me in a Coffee Shop? Seriously, go. I will be fine, I won't move"

He paused, nodded and strode out leaving Sarah alone. Actually alone. Other than a guy outside scribbling on some bits of paper, there was only her. She wrapped the large tartan scarf around her and clasped her hands around the warm Latte the waitress had just delivered. She shivered. Sitting back her mind drifted, where was she? Had she been here before? Who was Tom? People milled in and out again, having drank their drinks and all the while Sarah sat, willing the memory of Tom back again. She could see the reflection of the waitress walking away on the phone screen. She bolted upright, picked up the phone and pressed the button at the bottom. The screen illuminated. A woman keeps her life in a phone right? She pressed the green icon with a bubble. No messages. *Hmmmm* she thought. She then pressed a similar green icon with a white phone. Empty. *That's weird.* She clicked onto a colourful Spirograph. No Photos. Nothing. *What about contacts, there must be contacts* and she was right there were, five.

John

Macy

Eric

Someone called Rita and someone called John Snr.

"Who would only have five contacts?" she whispered.

"Would you like anything else?" the waitress asked as she passed looking at the now iced cold remnants of Sarah's latte.

"Hmmm? Oh no, no thanks" Sarah turned the phone over and over in her hand.

"Everything ok?" the waitress nodded at the phone "I.T issues?" she smiled.

"Oh this, yea maybe. Its, well...its empty"

"Empty?"

"Yea"

"Have you deleted your history?" the waitress asked,

"I don't think so? How would I know that?"

"You would know, as you would have to do it!"

Sarah shook her head.

"Restored to factory settings?"

Sarah stared blankly at the young blonde girl, with the nose piercing before her and shrugged. The girl laughed "Do you mind if I take a look? I'm pretty good with those things"

"Er...sure" Sarah answered and she handed her the phone. Once the tray was securely between her knees the girl started tapping away. The door opened with a small ring of a bell.

"Kathryn get that I'm busy" the blonde waitress shouted to the older woman behind the counter "Hey mind if I sit? This may take a minute"

"No not at all" Sarah moved up, the waitress took a seat only taking her eyes from the phone to place down the tray. About two minutes of clicking and swiping later the girl held it out to Sarah "Been wiped"
"Wiped?"
"Yea, cleared of all data"
"Why?"
"Well, that I can't tell you, but I can tell you when...sixth of September at 11:08am to be precise"
"How do you know?" Sarah gasped,
"I'm studying technology as a degree, actually technology engineering. Believe me I know. I can navigate a measly Iphone"
Sarah sighed, dropping back against the sofa. "You want your data back lady?" the waitress asked.
"What? I can get it back?"
"Yeah, it'll cost ya though. I have some hardware at home that can retrieve it. Nifty little thing, my mates ask me to unlock things on their boyfriends phones all the time, losers! I mean if you're gonna be with someone you gotta trust them right?"
"Erm...right, yea" Sarah s mind raced.
"So data, want it or not?" she got up and grabbed her tray,
"Yes!"
At that moment Sarah noticed John in the distance striding towards the coffee shop. Her heart pumped louder. "Erm, not now though, can I come back?"
The girl shrugged "Alright, I work Monday, Wednesday, Fri...."
"Great thanks"
John spotted Sarah and smiled as their eyes met through the glass "It will cost th...."
"No problem, what's your name?" Sarah interrupted without taking her eyes, or her smile, from her approaching husband.
"Ariel"
The door jingled "Ok Ariel, I will be in touch" Sarah whispered standing to grab her bag, she shot John a large smile,
"Hi, good meeting?" Sarah walked over to him, ignoring Ariel, who shrugged, shook her head and headed back to the counter.
"Who's that?" John smiled,
"Oh just the waitress, we were... just chatting"
"Oh about anything in particular?"
"No, nothing. The weather, all that, shall we go?"
Sarah grabbed his arm steering him out of the coffee shop and away from Ariel, who had now become her key to something. What that something was, Sarah wasn't sure, but she was sure if it was important enough to be deleted. It was important indeed.

Chapter 8

"Wanna come round to mine while we are off next week, prank phone call some of the college muppets?" Leah asked scoffing a strawberry lace.
"Cant. We are going away, to help mum 'find herself'" Macy rolled her eyes.
"Oh word, where?"
"Back to Malta, where the weather maybe better than this at least!" Macy pulled up her hood as the rain began to splodge on her hair.
"Where the fuck is this bus? Thought it was rubbish the last time you went, surely your dad doesn't want your mum to remember that!"
"Yea, but I think he's just hoping any memory is better than none, even if it's of them screaming at each other"
"Jeez, happy memories right there, when you going?" Leah's mouth still full of sweets.
"Tonight after dad picks up Eric from school, here's the bus, quick stick your arm out" Macy laughed as she shoved Leah out from under the shelter of the bus stop and into the shower.
"Fuck, Macy ya bitch, just got a raindrop right in the eye!" Leah danced,
"Oh stop complaining, I'll make you at hot chocolate with marshmallows at mine if you stand in the rain to flag it down" Macy chuckled.
"You drive a hard bargain, but....fine. Seriously though, one of us needs to pass our test. Fuck buses."
"Yeah, Fuck buses" Macy grinned.

The bus stopped only a few hundred feet from the gate to her house, but before they even stepped off Macy had spotted the car in her driveway. The woman standing by the buzzer was covered in a rain mac, she fought a few lose stands of brilliant red hair being blown into her face. Macy's heart began to race.
"Hey" she shouted "Hey"
"What the fuck?" Leah jumped,
Following her friends gaze she too noticed the woman, and as Macy began to stride towards her Leah had to quicken her step to keep up. There was a brief look between the woman in the mac and Macy before the woman quickly opened her car door.
"No wait" Macy yelled breaking into a run. The woman scrambled in, losing her hood, releasing her bright curls that now billowed out around her. She slammed the door and wheel span away moments before the girls reached her.
"What was that all about?" Leah asked breathlessly as caught up. "She shot off at the sight of you!"

Macy didn't answer, instead she did the only thing she could think of, memorise the number plate to the silver BMW tearing away down the road. Not that she was sure it would help, but for some reason she felt it was important.

"Come on Leah, let's go in" she started, turning and punching in the number that snapped the gate into life keen to retreat to the sanctuary of her home.

"She's not gonna ram the gate Mace" Leah said noticing the way Macy kept glancing back at the closing gate behind them,

"I know!" she snapped pulling her backpack up "I'm just checking"

"What's going on?"

"Nothing! Well I'm sure it's nothing. But honestly, I don't know"

They walked the rest of the way up to the house in silence, Leah knew Macy needed time to process something, she had seen that look on her friends face before. The way her brow furrowed and a small crease appeared between her eyebrows, how the she pursed her lips tightly causing them to turn down slightly at the corners. But mostly the way she stared with such determination straight ahead. It took them only six minutes to reach the front door and on opening the house, it was a hive of activity.

"Just let Marcia and Clarissa do their jobs honey, they always pack for us" her father was saying,

"I just don't feel comfortable, strangers packing my underwear"

John laughed aloud at his wife's struggle and Macy entered just in time to witness her mother playfully hit her father on the arm.

"Don't make fun of me" she blushed,

"Oh sweetheart, ok. No problem, you go upstairs and pack anything you want and I will inform Marcia and Clarissa of the situation" he still smiled as he turned to spot the girls "Ah, Macy glad you are back, I'm off to get Eric can you help your mother pack?"

"Pack?" Macy asked,

"Yes darling, your mother packs now" he teased.

"Hey!" Sarah chuckled "I just want to pack my own case, what is wrong with that?"

"Absolutely nothing Mrs R, you pack away" Leah offered heaving her college bag on the kitchen island where she took a seat "You look good by the way, I expected..."

"Leah!" Macy stopped her before, well anything crazy, came out of her friends mouth "Mum, this is Leah"

"Hi Leah nice to meet you" Sarah smiled,

"Technically we met like a bazillion times already but..."

"Leah!" Macy rolled her eyes at her friend again.

"What?!" she asked a mouth full of apple that she had taken from the bowl on the counter,

"Its fine, don't worry" Sarah offered kindly "If you don't mind girls I will go and pack"

"Would you like me to help when I get back, I won't be long?" John offered igniting surprised looks from the two teenagers.

"You help pack?" Macy blurted out in a chuckle,

"What?" John asked with mock hurt and a huge smile for his daughter.

"That would be lovely, I may need help navigating that wardrobe room thing" Sarah smiled back as she left them.

"Well Mace looks like it's not just your mum that changed" Leah chuckled.

"I pack!" John gloated

"Yeah you pack dad, course"

"Well I can if I want, I just choose not too" he grinned "why do something you can pay someone to do better"

"Is that how you became a gazilionaire?" Leah laughed,

"Something like that Leah, and you should take heed my dear, an old man like me can teach you a thing or two! Now if you girls will excuse me, I'm off to get Eric and then I will be home to help your brilliant mother pack her own case" he grabbed his keys and headed through the door to the garage.

"Wow they seem different, happy even" Leah noted as Macy heaved open the fridge and grabbed two cans of coke for them both.

"Yeah, strange isn't it? But it's nice"

"Don't you feel like you are betraying her?"

"Maybe" Macy turned her eyes down, yanking open the can with a fizz,

"What are you going to do?"

"Nothing"

"Nothing?"

"They seem to be enjoying each other"

"Yeah only because your mum can't remember anything"

"Well maybe that's a blessing in disguise" Macy mumbled before taking a long swig of coke.

The photo stared back at her. No denying that was her Sarah Ryan it said so right there by the grace of Her Majesty the Queen. She continued to stare at the passport until the heavily made up lady on the counter repeated her request for it

"Oh sorry" Sarah handed it over as John placed a concerned arm around her shoulders and gently rubbed her arm for comfort. She smiled up at him feeling more secure in his arms, it caused a slight flutter in her stomach.

"Ok Mr Ryan, you and your family can go straight through to the lounge, your plane is fuelling and will be ready in thirty minutes" her face beamed as she handed the four passports back to the tall, handsome man before her. He smiled kindly, retrieved the documents and without a second look at the check in lady he tightened his arm around Sarah and laid a soft kiss on the top of her head. The lounge was exquisite. Sarah gasped as she entered. If ever she had been in a five star hotel this must be what is was like. Large cream tiles snaked a walkway through the plush cream carpet like a shimmering river. In the distance water cascaded down a gold tiled wall and the sound was accompanied by soft music, offering a tranquil oasis to the harsh concrete exterior of the runway. Eric lead them to a group of sofas, his head phones denying him the acoustic pleasure, and plonked himself down without even removing his back pack. Sarah followed with her mouth hanging open until Macy asked,

"You ok Mum?"

"This is beautiful, do we always come here?" she whispered.

"Yes mum" Macy laughed "Dad always has a jet on hand"

"A jet?!" Sarah gasped this louder than expected John turned,

"You ok honey?"

"You have a jet?"

"Well, technically the business has a jet, but yes we always fly on it"

"Oh wow" Sarah slumped into one of the plush chairs as a woman appeared to take a drinks order. John sat next to her and took her hand.

"I work hard to give us all a good life" he muttered to her, quiet enough for her ears only "I will look after you if you let me?"

Sarah looked down at their joined hands. She had become accustomed to the weight of the three rings on her finger but was yet to be unimpressed by their sparkling glory.

"Will you let me?" he asked his eyes imploring hers, Sarah smiled and nodded.

"I'm going for a walk" Sarah said placing the sunglasses over her eyes to block out the vibrant Maltese sun.

"Ok honey, do you want me to come?" John shouts from the pool throwing Eric into the air, the sound of his laughter gurgles away as he lands in a huge splash.

"No thanks, I'll be ok, you three stay here"

"Will you be ok?" John's eyes narrow,

"Yes, yes, don't fuss..."

"I could come?" offers Macy resting the green book she had ben immersed in on the edge of her sun lounger.

"No thanks, honest, I will be fine. I will watch where I am going. I just, could do with some air"

"Well ok, if you are sure?" John smiles,

"I'm sure. Thank you"

She wasn't sure why she had added the last part of her sentence so she shook her head and swiftly left the villa. The cream limestone house nestled in a olive grove, surrounded by a high matching wall, was on the outskirts of Mellieha Bay, she had never been to Malta, so she needed to commit each step down the uneven warm concrete to memory. It didn't take long for her to reach the bustling centre. The red topped, three domed church cast its majestic far reaching shadow across the uneven streets of the sandy stoned town below. As she glanced skyward to the bright expense of blue and breathed in the sweet air, the church bells chimed into life, the echo swimming round the narrow passage ways littered with high multi-coloured enclosed balconies. It was midday. The sun will become hotter now. Almost unbearable for her virgin skin. Rounding a smooth bend Sarah spotted a small traditional cafe lined with wooden tables, shaded under a welcoming purple and white awning. She chose a seat that gave her the best view of the now few people passing. The town seemed to be going to sleep.

She was laughing as she ran into the restaurant her hair wet from the rain,
"I'm so sorry I'm late, fucking traffic, I hate this town!"
The two of them embraced, the aroma of the perfume she bought her for Christmas filled her nostrils.
"Don't worry, you're here now!"
"You know all London's good for?" the flamed haired woman asked "Traffic and rain Ava, traffic and bloody rain. Let's get a hot drink! I need it..."
"I ordered us Mochas"
"Great" she answered shaking through her hair in an attempt to dry it "so what's up?"
"It's Tom. He thinks I'm having an affair"
"Fuck me Ava, let me get my coat off before you drop that on me!" She gasped,
"Someone keeps calling the house. What am I going to do Gabrielle? He won't listen to me"
"Well firstly tell me everything" Gabrielle smiled.

GABRIELLE. She had almost choked on the memory, her mouth hung open.
"Sarah?"
She looked up, startled. The older woman standing before with short blonde hair and a heavy accent repeated, "Sarah! Sarah!"
"Erm. Excuse me do I know you?"
"It's me, Maria!" The lady laughed "I'm so happy to see you! I heard there had been an accident!" she slid into the seat opposite Sarah "Vincenzo" she shouted "It's Sarah! Come, get her a coffee". A petit, greying man appeared out of the door way, his broad smile revealed a caring face, his subsequent embrace was warm and friendly but Sarah was still confused.
"Sarah! Welcome back we have missed you! We heard about the accident" Vincenzo greeted loudly
"Yes, yes we are getting to that, the coffee eh Cenzo?"
The elderly couple exchanged some sharp sentences in Maltese before the man shuffled off back into the cafe muttering "Tajjeb, tajjeb Maria" as he went.

"So tell me dear, how are you?" Maria tenderly enquired.

"Erm. Well. I seem to have lost my memory, kind of" was this even the right explanation Sarah thought,

"My goodness mela!" Maria exclaimed, her hands clasped to her mouth "All of your memory?"

"Well not quite. It's complicated. But I'm afraid I have no recollection of Malta, or you...I'm sorry!"

"Not so worry my dear" Maria patted her hand but Sarah could have sworn she witness the tinge of relief in the lady's eyes. Vincenzo returned with a tray, on which stood a large carafe of coffee and three trembling cups.

"Stena Vinny" Maria said getting up taking the tray from him. Neither of them could have been more than five foot, milling over the tray together they looked happy and content. She lay out the table and as Vincenzo sat removing his apron Maria poured the coffee. "Sarah has lost her memory" Maria told him "Eh?"

"It's super complicated" Sarah interjected,

"Maybe for the best eh" Vincenzo sighed.

"What do you mean?" Sarah asked, surprised by his response.

"No" Maria snapped shooting him a look and continuing her chastising of her husband in a tirade of Maltese,

"Please wait, do you have something to tell me?"

They both looked at Sarah, taking in the vulnerability of their young friend. The turmoil bubbled inside Maria, maybe they were making a fresh start she thought, is it wise to tell her. The bell on the door chimed as a family emerged well fed into the warm winding street "Thank you" they shouted over, both their hosts rising to see them off leaving Sarah to consider their exchange. She took a gulp of her coffee, it burned her throat, things don't cool as quickly in this heat, she must try to remember. She watched the pleasant exchange in front of her, Maria however, looked smaller still, as if something weighed her down. A few more tourists entered and with an apologetic nod and wave and a promise to return soon, Vincenzo and Maria disappeared inside to attend to them. Frustrated Sarah reached down into her bag to pull out her phone. The screen lit up with a text from John.

Where are you?

She hadn't been gone long, but with the absence of a watch she couldn't be sure exactly, maybe only an hour or so, he really did worry, he must love her. She punched in a reply.

Just having a coffee in the sun. everything is ok. I can remember my way back.

She pondered over adding an X as a kiss to the end of the text but pressed send without it. Moments later the phone vibrated in her hand.

Where? I will join you?

Sarah smiled. The thought of him here was enticing, after their date she was intent on spending some more time with her 'husband' and this seemed like the perfect place. Whatever the kind couple wanted to tell her was in the past. She sent him the name and settled back down to people watching. The blackness of the phone against the white tablecloth soon got her thinking. Picking it up she turned it over and over in her hand. Her foot tapped against the gravely pavement. Something wasn't right. Thoughts of Ariel drifted in along with the salty sea air. Her phone had been wiped, but by whom? Should she ask John? He was her husband after all. Maybe he had done it to save her from things she didn't need to remember. That wasn't what was off though, something else was puzzling her and she couldn't put her finger on it.
"Sorry Mela" Maria cried out as she eventually reappeared without her husband "Lunchtime!"
"Don't worry" Sarah smiled,
"How are the children?" Maria's face lit up.
"Oh yes, good. They both seem great" Sarah answered with as much mothering instinct as she could muster.
"They are here with you now?"
"Yes back at the house, in the pool"
Maria laughed gleefully "He always loved the sea, Eric. We used to take him and Macy for days out on Vincenzo boat, all of us, all of you."
"You did?"
"Of course!" Maria beamed "Your children are like my children Sarah"
It didn't surprise Sarah, the warmth radiated from both her small hosts and she, even after a few minutes, could already feel an attachment. "You must come, tomorrow, bring them for lunch. They love my Lampuki and Cenzo potatoes, we make it tomorrow, today is all gone"
"Great" Sarah grinned finishing her coffee,
"You want another drink?"
"Wine" a strong voice interjected and Maria jumped.
"John! You're here quick" Sarah stood to greet him his arms wrapping round her in a tender embrace. She felt the heat of his open palm on the middle of her back and her body tingled in response.
"Hello Maria" John added,
"John" Sarah thought she witnessed a darkness flash over Maria, as quick as it came her smile returned.
"Sit, sit! For you both I will bring wine, and some food?"

Sarah's stomach grumbled, in the need to uncover her truth she kept forgetting to feed herself. She tossed the phone in her bag, the puzzle could wait till later, and she sat back the aroma of garlic filling her nostrils.
"Oh yes please Maria, food would be great"

John held her steady as she giggled her way up the winding street. Wine and heat were a heady mix and Sarah was unstable on her feet. He laughed at her calf like balance, and the smile it brought to her now carefree face. She had not looked this happy for a long time he thought, and it was nice to get a moment with his wife.
"What are you looking at?" she slurred,
"You" he said.
She burst into laughter "John Ryan, don't be trying to seduce me with those very, exceptionally, sexy eyes. It won't work" she tossed her head back as she laughed, he noticed the sunlight shone brightly on her exposed neck.
"My eyes are sexy?" he grinned,
"Shut up" she chuckled, losing her footing she stumbled dropping into his open arms "Whoa Sarah, be careful"
"Oooohhhhhh" she sang "My hero"
Entranced in her amusement he wrapped a secure arm around her waist, not wanting her to fall again and almost carried her back to the villa, beaming. As they approached the gate to the house she flopped up against the wall turning to look at him
"I love those two, Maria and Vinny, they're special." she slurred "You're very strong to carry me" she tried to enunciate each syllable and failed,
"You don't weigh that much" he smiled and it was true, at just over five foot four and slim, and John towering over six foot at her best guess, she must weigh almost nothing to him. Reaching in the back pocket of his navy linen shorts to find the key he could sense her gaze resting on him, she shifted to steady herself.
"Kiss me"
"What?" he asked,
"Kiss me!" she staggered towards him "I'm your wife apparently, so...Kiss me"
He could smell the wine on her sweet breath, her familiar deep brown eyes staring up at him. "Kiss me" she mouthed "Kiss your wife". Sarah smiled at the word
It caught him of guard. He took a moment to look down at the woman propping herself up against his chest. He felt the desire flare in him, the familiar shift in his groin as the blood rushed down declaring his lust.
"Please?" she breathed,
He felt the weight of her against him. She was drunk, beautifully drunk. His head tilted, his brows creased together and then he grabbed her, his lips bearing hungrily down on hers. He had made his decision in an instant.

John sat on the roof terrace, a glass of wine in one hand, a cigar in the other. She had looked utterly vulnerable, the sprawl of her dark hair in sharp contrast to the crisp white linen. She had groaned and grumbled when he gently laid her onto the large bed, but quickly fell into a deep alcohol induced slumber. He watched her for a moment, the rise and fall of her chest, the way her eyelashes softly brushed her cheeks. She looked happy. He quietly removed her flip flops and covered her with the Aztec blanket they had bought on a trip to Marrakesh for their tenth wedding anniversary, and kissed he forehead before retreating out of the room. There was no denying his carnal interest had been stoked but it wasn't how he wanted it to be, their first time since the accident. The smoke circled up to the star filled night sky as he exhaled.

"Dad?" Macy climbed the stone side steps that lead from the pool to the terrace and broke into his thoughts. "Eric and I are going to watch a film, do you want to join us?"

He pondered over his daughter's question, weighing up solitude over innocent laughter. "No thanks Macy I'm going to relax up here for a while"

"Should we wake mum? She's been out all afternoon!"

He saw the shine of her teeth as she smiled.

"No. Let her sleep, she's had a rough few months"

Macy slipped into the large cushioned seat next to her father tucking her legs underneath her and covering them with the navy fabric of her long cotton dress

"Do you think she will ever remember?" she asks.

Her father exhaled another trail of misty smoke leading to the heavens,

"We may have to accept that she won't, ever. At least she's safe, that's what we have to be thankful for" he smiled and patted her leg.

"That's true. But don't you think she seems different..." Macy ventured.

John sat up slightly in his seat "What do you mean?"

"She's, I don't know, more carefree, if that's the right word. Things that would have bothered her before don't seem to faze her"

"Like what?"

"Well last week I forgot my keys, she let me in without a word, in fact she smiled. And when Eric spilt milk down himself before we left on Friday, she just mopped it up. I mean, mum, mum would have gone mad...At both" Macy adjusted her gold arm bangle.

"That's not exactly worrying Macy" he laughed,

"No! But, I don't know, I can't put my finger on it. Something is off"

"Macy, she was hit by a car and took a heavy head injury, things will be different"

"Yea but..."

"That's enough" he snapped making Macy jump. She stared wide eyed at her father.

"Ok!" she exclaimed, rising.

"Macy" he groaned
"No its fine" she answered defensively, sauntering off "I'm going to watch a film with Eric"
He let her go. He didn't want to encourage her suspicion. Tonight, under this fresh twinkling black sky, he needed to focus his energy. He wasn't going to fail so soon.

Her mouth was dry, she was suffering a pounding behind her eyes. The room was in complete darkness. Fumbling around she flicked on the lamp on the bedside table
"Morning sexy" Tom grinned rolling over to face her "Good night?"
She made some faint grumbling noise "What time is it?"
"Seven, you're up early"
"I need to sleep. After water, I need water" she croaked
He rose out of the bed, the darkness of his skin glistening. His long legs were thick with fine Jamaican muscle, as his grandmother called it. He padded out of the room, returning with a large glass of, what looked to her, like liquid treasure, and paracetamol.
"Here baby, take these" She took them gladly from his open hand,
"Why do I always end up like this when I go out for one?!"
"I have one word for you, Gabrielle! The two of you are lethal" he laughed.
"You think we would know better, two grown women"
"I think you're both a bit slow baby" he chuckled kissing her exposed shoulder before sliding back under the duvet. Her mobile shrilled next to her,
"What the fuck" she said pills still between her lips. Tom grabbed it.
"Gabrielle" he smiled "Probably still pissed"

Sarah fumbled around in the dark, determined. She had woken with not only a fresh memory, but the realisation of what had been bothering her all day. As she attempted to shuffle to the end of the bed, sitting upright caused her to put her hand swiftly to her head and pause for a moment to let the room settle, she got tangled in something heavy, a blanket. She freed herself and tossed it on the floor. "Ouch" she muttered standing. The dizziness came with shooting thuds. It took her a minute, with limited light, to unsteadily bump along the wall feeling her way to flick on the light switch. Her bag sat by foot of the bed, in an instant she fell to her knees to retrieve her phone. The face illuminated. She swiped at it, opened the call history. Empty. It was unnerving. Who, she thought, had a wiped phone that never rang.

Chapter 9

The five of them laughed freely, exchanging memories of the summers before. Eric snorted so hard a piece of potato flew out of his nose, sending him even further into the giggles. Sarah sat back, her large rimmed sunglasses fending off the bright afternoon. She sipped at her water wishing the thudding behind her eyes would cease.

"That was so funny" Macy chuckled "I miss our summers out here Maria"

"I know dear, I know" she patted Macys hand across the table "Maybe you can come again next summer?"

Macy looked expectantly at her father,

"Yea of course, it will be good for your mum too" he glanced over at Sarah who hadn't said a word for a while

"Of course!" Vincenzo exclaimed "It's your home Sarah, you tell us all the time. Coming back here, well, it will make you happy again" he smiled, lifting his face so the skin gathered around his warm, trusting eyes. Sarah could only mirror his cheer weakly in return. Last night she had remembered Tom, almost clearly. His fiery hazel eyes sharp in contrast against his dark skin. She momentarily felt the complete comfort of the upturn of his plump lips, his smile revealing brilliant white teeth. Seconds before her mind could grasp the memory in its entirety she had been once again harshly betrayed by herself. Lying in bed with Tom was real. She knew it. She knew it in the way her stomach churned each time she desperately reached back for the dream, the way her heart filled with even the blurred lines of him, but there was something else. Another feeling she couldn't put a finger on, it didn't make any sense and it had plagued her all morning.

"What do you think mum?" Eric's voice brought her back to reality,

"Hmmm?"

"If we all go swimming?"

"Now?" she looked around to the small restaurant brimming with people. Through the busy tables, the noisy chatter, the clinking of glasses and clatter of cutlery a woman sat alone, her face up to the sun. Sarah couldn't help but notice how the sun glistened all the way down her sleek blonde hair. Her hands lay clasped together in her lap. She appeared motionless until slowly her eyes opened and her head turned to meet Sarah's stare. The woman smiled broadly, it caught Sarah off guard. All she could do was sit up and turn away. That's when she noticed the man in the white linen shirt striding confidently toward the woman, he slid a gentle hand over her shoulder as he passed to take his seat opposite and picked up the menu, chatting animatedly to her. Sarah's gaze returned to the woman, who still looked at Sarah, but had since lost the smile completely from anywhere other than her mouth. Sarah's stomach dropped.

"I'm just going to the bathroom" Sarah mumbled.

"Are you ok honey?" John took her hand "You look pale"

"Hangover" Macy giggled and winked at her mother,

"I'm fine" Sarah rubbed the top of Johns hand before he took her wrist and softly kissed the inside without taking his eyes from his wife's. The tender moment caused a hush at the table and Sarah felt her cheeks burn. "I won't be long."

She splashed cold water in her face to revive herself and stared into the mirror above the sink. Her eyes appeared tired, her skin slightly darker, her long thick hair scratched at the bareness of her back. She scooped it up into a bun at the top of her head, releasing the irritation. The door opened and she spotted Maria in the mirror, behind her.

"My dear, how are you?" Maria asked. She was a woman of age, having four grown children and six grandchildren of her own, Maria was good at reading people. She had had to be.

"I'm ok" Sarah sighed,

"Are you remembering things?" Marias eyes searched hers.

"Maybe"

Maria gulped. She felt her face drop and chastised herself for being so transparent, forcing the smile quickly back into situ she ventured "What things Mela?"

Sarah played with the sunglasses in her hand.

"Was I bad?" she looked expectantly at Maria,

"No! No! Why do you say this?"

"I don't know..."

"Oh my darling girl" Maria hugged her "You are the mostly lovely wife, mother and friend, you didn't deserve..." She stopped, once again punishing herself internally.

"Wait, what? Deserve what?"

"Nothing, nothing" Maria waved her hands.

"Maria?"

Her shoulders dropped "I don't know. Ok. You never said. Only you came to us, Vinny and I last summer, in a mess. You said you wouldn't be coming back for a while..."

"What? Why?" Sarah's ears filled with the sound of her own racing pulse.

"I don't know! You wouldn't say. But, you got a flight home yourself... and you..."

"I what? Please tell me" Sarah begged

"You had a, what do you call it. Black eye. Bruises. Everywhere."

Sarah staggered back, catching herself on the sink to save her legs from collapsing under her. "What? What happened?" she whispered, but Maria only shrugged

"Was it, John?" she gasped,

"I don't know mela. Maybe. I only know that he was kind and loving to you and then, something changed"
The bathroom seemed to swirl around Sarah. Was this her fault? The memory of Tom, had she done this? The door flung open and a beaming Macy strode in. Sarah stood upright instantly, ignoring the tremble throughout her body that threatened to buckle her legs at any moment.
"Everything ok?" Macy ask looking uncertainly between the two women.
"Yes fine Habibi, we are going back now" Maria stroked the girls face and gently pulled Sarah out into the bright, busy restaurant,
"Come Sarah, I shouldn't have said anything. Everything is ok now no?"
Sarah nodded slightly but her eyes, still wild darted around the busy room, Maria pulling her forward when her body felt like it was being pulled back, as if an invisible elastic band connected her to the bathroom, to before she knew this. Sarah slid awkwardly into the chair next to John, careful not to touch him as she did. He turned to her, a broad innocent smile spread across his face. She replaced her sunglasses and sat back and watched his brow furrow,
"Ok darling?" he enquired.
"Yes of course" she croakily answered.

The sea was warm and surprisingly clear. The view extended all the way down to the rocky seabed deep beneath his feet. But he knew this already, he had swum in this greeny blue elixir a thousand times. The children could just be heard splashing and teasing each other over the swill of his arms as he treaded water. He was watching them all. Macy and Eric running in the waves, Vinny holding tight on to Maria as she paddled through, pointing and shouting some kind of warning to Eric before a wave crashed into him and he fell backwards, John stopped. Sinking slightly, not taking a breath until he saw the smiling face of his son scramble back to his feet unharmed and the momentary danger had passed. He looked to her. She hadn't moved. Not even in the tiny fragment of time where their son had been washed over, she hadn't even flinched. He treaded. She gazed out passed them, passed him, all the way out over the ocean lost in her own world.
"Can you pass me the towel" He asked her when he eventually returned to the rocks.
"Oh, yes of course"
He noticed her avert her eyes and the shot of colour warming her cheeks. He smiled to himself. Wrapping the towel round his waist he flicked his hair back and took a seat close to her "Everything ok?" he asked.
"Will you stop asking me that" she grinned,
"Sorry, I can't help it. I want to make sure you are happy" he felt her tense beside him and caught the pause in Maria's step in the distance as she spotted them "Have I missed something?" he looked at Sarah.

She pulled her knees up to her chest and covered them with her dress "No. Why would you ask that?"

"It's, just you seem, anxious. And I thought we were getting closer" he dropped his head causing her stomach to do the same. He seemed a good man. She studied his face as he looked up to watch Eric. The tiny blonde hairs that shone in the sun. Surely you can tell a lot by how a man fathers his children and he was patient and kind. They adored him. Could he really have hurt her?

"We are" she offered "but I'm still trying to work a few things out"

"May I put my arm round you?" he asked tenderly.

She paused for a moment before nodding as he lifted a muscly arm over her head and pulled her into him, he smelt of the sea. She felt him dust a light kiss on the top of her head.

"I do love you Sarah" he whispered but she didn't know how to answer and so they sat in silence listening to the wave's crash, interrupted only by the distant sound of an occasional car horn.

"You promise to call this time?" Maria whispered to Sarah in the airport terminal

"I promise"

"We will worry, Vinny and I" both women looked over to Vinny currently embracing the children, a proud smile on his face "They are like our grandchildren" Maria sighed "And you, our daughter"

"Thank you, both. It was great to meet you, well see you. You know what I mean" they laughed together "I will call so much you will be sick of me"

"You have our number in the phone?"

"Absolutely" Sarah grinned holding the phone tight to her chest *now I have six contacts* she thought.

"Good"

"Right everyone, let's go. Vinny, Maria, wonderful as always. Thank you so much" John hugged them both "You are welcome over to us anytime you know?" he offered,

"Thank you son" Vinny answered "We come when the rain stops"

"In that case never" Macy laughed.

"You know me Macy my dear. Made for the sun" Vinny answered her,

"Made for nothing" Maria laughed patting his staunch belly, many years of tenderness lay in that one jest.

"Ah that's it" he answered winking at his petite wife.

"Next time can we get the boat out?" Eric asked enthusiastically,

"Of course! And then I teach you to be a great sailor...and drink rum" Vinny whispered the last part,

"Maybe hold off on the alcohol" John chortled "We really do have to go"

Sarah and Maria realised they were still holding onto each other, smiling weakly as they relinquished their grip. Both hearts quickened. Each one feeling the falter of their own stance but neither allowing the other to see.

"See you soon" Sarah croaked,
"Yes you will my dear" Maria declared.

Chapter 10

She was determined. Ever since they landed home over a week ago her only focus was this. It was all planned for today and she needed things to go smoothly.

There was a light knock at her bedroom. His face appeared in the crack of the door "Morning, can I come in?"

"Of course" she finished smoothing down the freshly made bed and stood upright "Everything ok?" Sarah ventured,

"Ah you're asking me that now!" he grinned "I'm off to work today. There's a board meeting I have to attend"

This wasn't news to her. "Are you sure you're going to..." he continued

"You're not going to say it are you?" Sarah laughed,

"Ok, ok!" he held his hands up in mock defeat "It's just, well my first full day, I won't be home till late and Macy is staying at Leah's tonight so you will be alone most of the day"

Perfect she thought. "I know John, I have a plan"

"A plan?" his head tilted,

"Yes, I'm planning to go into town and do some shopping. It will be Christmas before we know it and I would like to pick up some things, get organised. I think I know which pin goes with which card, so I may just, retail therapy my day...if that's ok?" she asked seeing his facial expression drop.

"Of course, of course. Actually I'm glad. It's good that you are getting back to normal". Normal. What did that mean she pondered, but only for a split second, she was much too busy today. "Really?" she ventured,

"Really" he answered his smile returning.

"I just wanted to ask one thing" she coughed "...Do I have a car?"

The need hadn't arisen before, John drove them everywhere and she hadn't actually needed to be anywhere until now.

"Yes!" he smirked "You have a car. Come on. I will show you"

She took his outstretched hand and followed him down the stairs and through the large door in the kitchen, the very one she walked through weeks ago as a stranger into this now not so strange life. He led her past his familiar Range Rover and the sporty sliver Mercedes through another door she hadn't even noticed before. He flicked on a light and dropped a bunch of keys into her hand.

"You normally drive that one. Automatic so you shouldn't have any problems" he grinned. Three motionless vehicles sat glittering before her. A large matt black matching Range Rover at which he had pointed. A sleek red, long nosed convertible and a blue Porsche. "Wowzers" she mumbled.

"Don't ever say I didn't treat you Mrs Ryan" he winked, beaming,

"That you did" she whistled,

"Honey I have to go, but be careful, if you take that one remember it's huge, a bugger to park! Which is not really your forte" he winked before continuing "That one is a classic so the drive will be heavy. But that one, that's fast as fuck, so choose wisely I don't want to have to worry about you even more" he laughed.

"Ok, duly noted" she grinned.

He paused for a moment, his briefcase hanging by his side. His eyes caught hers. He could see the amusement that had been dancing in them slowly dissipate. She held his stare looking down only to his lips, poised in a small upturn. He leaned closer, watching the muscles in her neck move as she swallowed. She didn't recoil from his kiss. In fact a bolt of something electric shot through her as their lips met and their mouths explored each other's. They had begun to kiss with some regularity now but each time was new and exciting. "I have to go" he smiled pulling away "Even if I don't want to"

The intimacy had woken something in Sarah, and her body tingled in parts that had lain dormant. She had relinquished the affection control to him since her drunken attempt to seduce him in Malta. Today's kiss had caused an unexpected ache for more.

"Um yes of course" she tucked her hair behind her ear and bit her lip. She could taste him. He didn't move. Laughing, she pushed at his chest "Go then"

"Ok I'm going" he answered, but he leaned in for another quick kiss before climbing into his car. She watched with interest, waving as he reversed out.

"Don't forget to choose wisely" he shouted back at her through his open window,

"I will" she shouted back and with that he sped off down their drive the wheels just turning out of sight as the garage door clicked shut.

Sarah shook her head, she must regain her focus. Running back to grab her bag and the important piece of paper it contained, she checked all the doors were locked before fobbing open the big car, remembering that was automatic, and climbing inside.

The car screeched into the same spot, the display reading 7:59 "Shit". Grabbing the briefcase from the passenger foot well he headed into the familiar building. Pushing through the glass doors into the empty atrium he was met by his PA running down the stairs.

"Everyone is here" she said "here are the documents and I have noted the main points on the first page". John took the files she held out to him in silence.

"How was Malta?" she enquired,

"Yea, fine"

"..And Sarah?"

"I don't have time right now ok, I have to get into this meeting"

His abruptness was like a smack in the face but she hid it well even though she had never quite got used to it, however that didn't allude to the fact that it wasn't unexpected. She straightened her back as he brushed passed her taking the stairs easily two at a time, and disappearing behind the swinging double doors.

Standing just around the corner of the bustling board room, ensuring he was out of sight, he took a moment to compose himself. Fiddled with his tie to ensure it was perfect and inhaled a couple of deep breaths. "John?"

He jumped "Jesus!"

"Sorry, I didn't mean to startle you" she held her hand up.

"What?" the impatience clear in his voice.

"Are you sticking around after the meeting?"

"Er, I'm not sure, why?"

"I just thought we could talk" she muttered "I have some things I need to go over with you"

He glared at her. This meeting was one of the most important in his entire career, no his entire life and she wanted 'to talk'.

"Now's is not a good time."

"When is it ever...." she sighed,

"Look I have a lot on my plate, work, the kids, Sarah" he saw her flinch at the name.

"I haven't forgotten" she insinuated,

"Well. I wish you would"

Suddenly the empty corridor in which they both stood felt icy and vast, anechoic. The meeting room door flung open and John's father strode out, his head high, his shoulders pushed back. "Son, we are waiting" he boomed glaring between the two of them.

"Yes, sorry father" and without a second look John Jr disappeared into the board room.

'You have arrived at your destination' Sarah drove round in circles squinting to see the address on the piece of paper she held in front of her, and looking for the numbers on the street. 24, 26, 28. "Found it" she uttered, now to find a space on this narrow terraced street, big enough for her to park. She regretted bringing 'The Beast' as she had affectionately named the car during their last two hours together. She would have to leave it at the end of the street. Reversing back Sarah rolled her eyes as the front end of the car behind her appeared on the screen in the middle of the dashboard.

"Course it has camera's, it has everything other than a kettle" she chuckled to herself. John didn't buy crap that's for sure. She reached for her bag, the mobile buzzing into life causing her to jump. "Shit"

The display read John

"Hello?"

"Hi Honey, it's me. Just calling to check if you are ok?"

"Yea fine" her voice shrilled higher than she expected, it startled her. She coughed "How are you? How was the meeting?"

"Oh you know, boring. Still going actually, just taking a quick break, so I thought I would call my hot wife"

She blushed even though she was alone "Thanks"

"So how much damage have you done?"

"What to the car?"

"No" he laughed "To the credit card!"

"Oh" she chuckled too "Nothing yet, I'm only just here"

"Oh right"

"I had a coffee after you left, milled around for a bit..." her heart drummed

"That's ok honey, I'm not checking up! You do what you like. Actually I'm hoping to get home at some sort of reasonable hour and I wanted to ask you something"

Her throat went dry "Anything..."

"Would you like to go on another date with me?" she could hear the smile in his voice.

"I would love that" she confessed,

"John...." Sarah heard the woman's voice call him in the background.

"Shit, look gotta go honey. Be ready for seven ok? I can't wait to see you"

"Ok, hope the meeting...." but he had gone.

For a moment she sat cocooned in the huge lump of metal. Her reflection appeared in the window, it struck her she must look like a woman with her wonderful life together. Her resolve faltered. He was her husband, and it was even starting to become enjoyable, this new life. She looked at the round Start/Stop button and considered driving away but she grabbed her bag, steadied her resolve and opened the door after all she had driven all this way and there were answers she needed to get, whether she wanted them or not. It took some incessant knocking, and a few double checks of the address before the door was finally answered. Her blonde hair was dishevelled, this time she had a dark black ring through her nose.

"Oh fuck, I forgot about you" Ariel mumbled through a yawn,

"Great!" Sarah answered.

"Oh don't get your knickers in a twist, come in, I will just get changed"

It was obviously student digs, given away by the bottles of beer that covered any surface, the half-eaten pizzas, a putrid smell coming from dirty pots in the sink and the cracked leather sofa that had possibly been manufactured before Ariel was even born. "Sit. I will be five" Ariel instructed.

Sarah pulled her bag closer, perching on the edge of the couch. The brown carpet being slightly sticky underfoot as she shifted her weight. What was wrong with the youth of today, Macy certainly wasn't going to live like this, she would make sure of that. The clock in the kitchen ticked through the silence.

"Right got the cash?" Ariel asked as she reappeared in some jeans and a white vest, her hair unchanged,

"Yes of course" Sarah rummaged in her bag and produced the envelope. Even this had been a struggle, to bring up bank accounts and pin numbers with John as nonchalantly as possible. He didn't seem to suspect anything though, Sarah must have had some indulgent months quite regularly before. The only surprising thing was the account balance. Sarah had gasped, the people behind her in the queue becoming suspicious so she grabbed the three hundred pounds and rushed back to her car before anyone could say anything.

"Looks like it's all there"

"It is" Sarah assured.

"Right, phone" Ariel held out her hand and Sarah placed the empty black box in her palm. "You take this one" She exchanged it with an identical handset "I have calibrated it to yours so all your texts, call etc will come straight through to this one and no one will be any the wiser"

"Ok" Sarah muttered inspecting the new identical device.

"It should take me a week, maybe two, depending on how far back you wanna go, and my shifts at that fucking coffee shop but I will drop you a text once it's done. I programmed my number in…"

"No! I can't have a strange number on there"

"Relax, I hid it"

"Oh right, you can do that?"

"Lady I can do anything with this piece of shit, it's as sophisticated as a kiddies toy"

"Ok. Well if that's everything?" Sarah rose to leave, the stench getting too much,

"Wait, before you go, why are you doing this? What do you want to know, because I can't control what you find, I tell this to everyone, I don't want you breaking down in tears and snorting on my shoulder, if you know what I mean" Ariel enquired.

"Does it matter?"

"I'm intrigued. Posh sort like you…."

"I lost my memory and I need to know if my husband is trustworthy" was a much as Sarah was prepared to share,

"Lady. They very rarely are" Ariel smirked.

His head thudded as he rubbed at his tired eyes causing the papers strewn out in front of him to blur for a few seconds. He wished they could stay that way. Only his desk light cut through the blanket of darkness that extended way beyond his vision. The night was clear. He could make out the twinkle of the stars on their nightly flirtation, the big beaming moon casting sharp shadows across the empty parking lot spread out beneath him. Squinting out through the window in the lone lit office, he felt something alien to him, insignificant.

"I didn't want to leave without seeing you"

"Fuck" John jumped round, his hand to his chest "You nearly gave me a heart attack"

"I told you I wanted to talk" she glided in, slinking down into the chair opposite his desk.

"And I distinctly told you, today wasn't a good day" he announced. She brushed smooth the grey skirt over her thighs picking off a small speck of fluff and turned her face up to him expectantly.

"Mabel, I really don't want to go over this tonight"

"How are things at home?" he saw the glint of fire in her heavy set brown eyes. He caught the glimmer of the bronze eyeshadow that adorned her lids. His gaze followed the thickness of the dark liner as it traced her lashes until it flicked out from the corners. The edge of her creamy lips turned up.

"I'm only asking because I care John" she purred.

"This is not happening anymore ok. Sarah is…"

"Sarah is what?" she snapped, those eyes burning into him, her mouth tightened.

John watched the snatch of her breath, the way her breathing heaved her bosom. He could trace the contours of her pert womanliness through the delicate fabric of her cream blouse. A tantalising peak of deep cleavage where the material crossed over, rising and falling.

"Sarah is home. She is back" he explained.

Mabel sat back in the chair, crossing one leg smoothly over the other "Is that so? For how long?"

"For forever ok Mabel, now this has to stop. What I told you, the things I said, what we did. You have to forget it"

"I don't *have* to forget anything" her leg bobbed, bouncing the black stiletto balanced on the end of her foot. She idly twisted her long, tight curled hair.

"Please May" he pleaded. She shot forward in her chair

"I'm doing this for you! To help you get out of there"

"I don't want to get out of there" he bellowed bringing his fist down onto the desk. This time it was her that jumped..

"But you said"

"I know what I said" He snapped "I know what I promised you" her eyes glistened "But I told you, forget it. Let it go"

"But, I … I can't"

"Well you have to and that's the end of it"

"How long have I known you John Ryan? How long have I been here adhering to your every whim. Ensuring you got everything you want and you think I can just walk away, after all this time? And let you play happy families like some delusional prick?"

"What do you want?" John opened the top drawer pulling out his cheque book "Come on May, name your price"

Her mouth fell open and tears stung her eyes. She blinked them away. "Fuck you John" and with that she rose and sashayed out of his office and into the darkness.

Chapter 11

His morning kiss had plagued her all day. Even sitting in that shithole house with Ariel wondering what had been hidden from her. Even rolling round her mind the possible reasons why she had bruising in Malta the night Maria mentioned, and more importantly who had given her them. The kiss was all she could focus on. The softness of his mouth on hers, the taste of his sweet intrusive tongue. She thought about other places on her he had used that to explore. The taste of rusty liquid interrupted her daydream, she had bitten through her lip.

"Hi honey, I'm home. Sorry I'm a bit late" she heard John shout from downstairs. She even heard the jangle of his keys as he placed them in the blue glass bowl in the hall way where she knew her keys already sat. "Are you ready?" he asked.

By his footsteps she knew he took the stairs two at a time. Her heart boomed through her chest. She had taken time to choose the electric blue dress that clung to her curves. There was even the excitement of discovering the dazzling display of lingerie she owned, picking out the black lace set the dress now hid. It doubled her assets, and put them proudly on display. Carefully she had pinned up her hair, drawing attention to her long smooth neck, allowing just a few falling curls. With, she was sure, the same detailed attention that Michelangelo applied to the Sistine chapel she had brushed on her makeup, keeping it soft but sultry. Yes that's what the lady in the shop had called it- sultry. Or was it slutty. Well too late now. She adjusted her pose, smoothed down her dress. Dusted of the nude suede stilettoes and standing in the middle of the room took a deep breath.

"Hey where are you honey?" he shouted,

"I'm in the bedroom" she replied, her voice catching in her throat.

"Nope…"

"Oh erm, *your* bedroom" she stammered. Each footstep got louder, rooting her to the spot, he appeared in the doorway.

"Holy fuck!" he exclaimed.

"Do I look ok?" Sarah smiled meekly,

"Ok? No, absolutely not ok, anything but ok. You look amazing. Gorgeous. Sexy as hell!" and for the second time this evening John eyes were drawn to the heave of a deep cleavage. Only this time it was his wife's.

"Thanks" she flushed, the vulnerability of her caused him to harden in his trousers.

"I, erm. Wow. I mean wow. I want to kiss you, so fucking bad right now"

Her legs didn't wobble anymore. Driven on by his reaction she strode over to where he still stood and leaned up slowly to place her lips on his. It was just as she remembered. Just as she hadn't stopped remembering all day. Her body lit up with instant fire, she felt her own nipples push out against the tightness of the lace on her bra. The attraction was fierce, the desire more so. His arms wrapped around her waist, hungrily pulling her against him.

"Welcome home" she muttered through his kiss,

"Welcome home indeed" He pressed his forehead against hers and beamed down at her "So, still want to go out or...?"

"Well I haven't got dressed for nothing" she smiled.

"Ok, just give me five mins, for a freezing cold shower, and I'm all yours"

She leaned up and kissed him again quickly "Ok but don't be long, I'm starving" she grinned.

The final credits of the film rolled up and so did the lights, the slow hum of human voices and shuffling from seats commenced.

"That was awesome!" Leah whistled "Daniel Craig is hot!"

"He's alright, not my type" Macy pulled a face,

"Not your type, what the hell's wrong with you girl!"

Macy laughed at her friend as she pulled the mobile from her pocket. "Shit I've missed three calls from Eric. Hope he's ok"

"Call him back" Leah offered.

"I will, but let's get out of here first".

The girls filed out behind the stragglers of viewers as the cinema staff with their sweeping brushes meandered in ready to clean the discarded popcorn, and empty sweet bags from the sticky aisles. As they were delivered from the darkness into the bright lights of the lobby Macy punch redial until she heard her little brother answer "Hey"

"Hey Ricardo, everything ok?" Macy asked softly, using the nickname she had given him as a toddler.

"Yeah kind of, I'm just a bit worried" he sighed.

"Worried about what bro?"

Leah made a gesture towards outside and mumbled something about a cab before pulling her pink and purple bobble hat over her head and disappearing off. Macy sat alone on one of the metal seats in the now deserted bar, it was well past last orders. "About Mum, and Dad"

"Ah. Well talk to me. What's worrying you?"

"Is he going to tell her Mace?" his voice was small, he was obviously trying not to wake his dorm mates but it was enough to feel like she had just been punched in the stomach. That question needed no explanation. Macy knew exactly what he was talking about. "I don't know" was all she could offer.

"Don't you think he should, like, all this pretending, this everything is fine nonsense? It's not right!"

"What do you suggest he does Eric? She's been through enough...and she's different. Better. Why would he try to ruin things for her? Or us? "

"Oh I don't know because she deserves to know Macy".
She pulled her jacket tighter against the sudden chill in the air "Eric, just leave it to dad"
"That woman's gonna keep coming back, and mum's going to find out through her and everything will come crashing down"
"Well no worse than before" Macy mumbled. The security guard approached her leaning down to tell her they were closing up and she needed to leave
"Listen, I have to go. Don't worry about things ok Eric. Dads got this covered, everything will be fine"
"Yeah until she remembers"
"Well then, we will deal with that, if it happens. Until then we don't say anything ok? Promise?" there was a moment of silence on the phone until Eric finally responded
"Fine. But only because I don't exactly know how to tell someone they were missing for six months anyway Mace"

They sat close, at a small wooden table at the front. Their legs pressed against each other, their hands clasped together resting on his thigh. The rings he had bought her glittered as the soft spotlight swept across them. She noticed him looking at them and smiled. He caught her eye in the dimness of this heady room and she felt him squeeze her hand. The woman finished her final note as the jazz gently drifted off. Everyone erupted into applause. Even in the intimate nature of the space, the few people that filled the wine coloured walls created quite a noise. But to no avail the encore was over and the woman in the gold dress drifted off the small, shell lit stage.
"Wow, that was amazing" Sarah finished clapping, a glow in her cheeks. He wasn't sure if it was the music or the red wine.
"We had our first date here" he told her, watching her reaction intently. Her eyes widened. "Really?" she gasped.
"Really. You hated it" he grinned.
"No! Not possible. How can anyone hate this place? It's exquisite. And the music, Oh god. It's so, sensual"
"Well you were seventeen" he laughed,
"Seventeen! That would have made you....?"
"Twenty four" he answered.
"I was going to say, a bit weird" she laughed.
"Ah well" he sat back and picked up his bottle of beer and leant back in his chair "That too. But in my defence you didn't look seventeen"
"How old did I look?" she asked her eyebrows raised.
"Seventy" he teased the bottle paused at his upturn lips. She hit him softly on his exposed forearm where he had rolled up the sleeves of his shirt.
"Why here?" Sarah asked leaning into him.

"You said you wanted me to take you somewhere you hadn't been before, so I asked if you liked Jazz and you pulled a face like this" he stuck out his tongue and grimaced "and so I figured you wouldn't have been here. But you hated it" he chuckled.

"I'm so sorry" She ran her hand up his arm and it sent waves of desire through him, "I love it now though" she offered with a smile.

"Good. Now is all that matters"

"How did we meet John?" she asked quietly.

"Ah! Well you fell."

"I fell? Oh god!" she groaned.

"...from heaven" he teased laughing and she rolled her eyes "No truthfully, you did fall. Obviously not from heaven but coming out of the college building. I was waiting at the lights and you stumbled down, I don't know, twelve stone steps"

"Oh how embarrassing" her cheeks flushed red.

"I jumped out of the car and ran to help"

"My real life hero" Sarah smiled.

"Actually you told me to, now wait, what were your words again, let me get this right, oh yea. 'Fuck off'" he smiled as the beer bottle touched his lips and he took another swig.

"No! That's awful"

"It was a bad day, I discovered" he averted his eyes,

"What do you mean?" Sarah enquired sensing the unease in her husband.

"Your father had just died. You were on your way to the hospital"

And there it hung between them, the horses kick to Sarah's stomach, the constricting guilt of John's revelation. How could she morn a father she couldn't remember. In fact she couldn't even remember a father at all. Not as Sarah or not as Ava. It was both disorientating and sickening.

"Would you like another drink?" he asked finishing the last of his beer. Sarah could already feel the warmth of the alcohol, she didn't want to risk another Malta, him having to put her to bed, and suddenly she needed to leave. To escape these four small walls that were closing in. She shook her head.

"Shall we get out of here then?" he offered to her relief. She nodded. "Ok, I'm just going to visit the little boy's room"

"I will wait outside"

She grabbed her coat and tying it quickly round the waist , picked up her bag and almost ran up the tiny stairwell as fast as the tight dress would allow, spilling her out into the crisp night air. Sarah fumbled around for her phone. She wanted to call anyone, text someone, just reach out. Where were her friends? Her family? Could there really be no-one missing her. Was she that insignificant? A tear fell down her cheek. She swiped it away. Opening her messages she responded to the last one Maria had sent

Weather is cold how about you?

Not much to report. No memories yet.
Will book hypnotherapy soon.
Love to you both x
She swiped at another tear and looked out across the empty back alley.

It was a quiet cul-de-sac lined with similar red brick semi's. His hand tenderly caressed her thigh as he pulled up and switched off the engine.
"You sure you're ready for this baby? They are a force to be reckoned with"
Taking his innocent face in both her hands she kissed him passionately.
"Ok now I'm ready" she smiled, tugging on the car door and climbing out. Tom followed, noticing the greeting party waving frantically through the window,
"There they all are baby, there's no going back now"
"Come on silly, it will be fun to meet your family"
"Yea, ya say that now"
She laughed, waved back to them, and took his outstretched hand waiting to be led inside. The yellow door opened before they had set foot on the pathway and quite a number of small children of differing ages spewed out.
"Uncle Tom!" came the calls as he scooped up a few of them and the rest he hi-fived,
"Hey you lot this is my friend Ava"
"Hi" she waved and smiled.
"Your girlfriend more like" one of the taller boys jibbed.
"Hey Parker, get inside" the boy ran at the sound "Tom, my boy come in, come in. You must be Ava?" the older lady with greying untamed hair held out her hand taking Ava's. She was dressed in traditional Caribbean clothing and the colours were beautiful, Ava thought. Yellow and purple. Her bangles jingled as she talked. "Come meet my family, we are blessed to welcome you"

"Sarah?" her head shot round to a puzzled looking John "You ok? You were miles away there"
"Sorry" she mumbled, eyeing the blackness of the screen on the phone she still held in her hand.
"Expecting a call?" he nodded to it, the familiar small line appearing between his brows.
"What? No. Just checking the, erm, time" she dropped it in her bag "shall we grab a cab?" she took his arm and steered him away as if he could see into the memory she so desired to protect. His pocket vibrated. He made no attempt to acknowledge the shrilling.
"Are you going to get that?" she asked. Darkness flashed across his face. "No" was all he said and by the tone Sarah already knew not to press further. The taxi ride was quiet and John headed straight upstairs when they arrived home. Sarah wandered into the kitchen and poured herself a glass of water.
Something had changed, and she didn't mean her memory. The sound of the

shower busting into life above her gave her a brief opportunity. Placing down the drink she slid out of her shoes and laying her coat on the chair she slowly crept up the stairs, her footing silent against the steps. Inching down the landing, the carpet sumptuous beneath her feet, she caught a final glimpse of a naked John clicking shut the en suite. She pushed open the door and scanned the bedroom. His jacket lay limply over a dresser chair. With her heart in her throat she forced herself to step as quietly and quickly as she could across the room and fumble through his pockets. The phone dropped to the floor. She shot a look up at the bathroom door. He was still showering. Crouching she snatched it up in her trembling hands, swiping it into life. The image of the children illumined her face. There was a passcode. She remembered back to the morning she showed her the photos. What was the code? Had she seen it? Could it be a date? Did she know any? It vibrated in her hand and she jumped, causing the handset to fly across the bed its loud, incessant ring echoing around her. *Shit.* Sarah launched across and grabbed it the screen lit up with one name. A name she recognised.

"Hello. Hello?"

She'd answered it by mistake. *Fuck.* The shower stopped. Sarah froze. There was something stuck in her throat. She couldn't swallow. His footsteps were heading for the door. Her heart pounded in her ears. She could hear him grab the doorknob. Shoving the phone back in his pocket, the handle on the en-suite door bent. She dived on the bed landing as seductively as she could. She smoothed down her dress, just as the door opened and a freshly showered John appeared.

"Sarah?" he glanced round the room in confusion his eyes resting on his jacket
"I thought maybe I could stay in here tonight" she tried to distract him hoping she had hidden the tremble in her voice. His eyes widened and for the first time since the bar the tightness of his expression fell and he managed a small smile.
"With me?" he asked,
"If you want?" her voice was small but expectant.
"If you are sure?"
"Yes" she breathed, her chest risings heavily. He paused. He was sporting only a towel around his waist. He ran his hands through his hair and after a momentary tilt of his head, he crawled gently up the bed to softly kiss his wife.

Chapter 12

"Clara can you please come in here a moment" he asked pressing the button on his phone. The double doors opened.

"Yes Dr Maxwell?"

"I've been looking for a file, Sarah Ryan, have you seen it? The Ryan family" Clara tilted her head and drummed her fingers where she still held the door. She strode over to the enormous mahogany filing cabinet and opened the top drawer.

"I checked there" he snapped. She swung round to observe him sat heavy in his chair. She folded her arms and raised an eyebrow.

"That's how you're speaking to me now?" she remarked.

"I need it. She hasn't even had a bloody follow up!" he boomed.

"I can send her a follow up if you like, I have her address on my computer" she offered,

"Fine. Summon her. I need to see this patient. Mark it urgent Clara, don't forget"

"Forget?" she admonished "you think I will forget Dr Maxwell?"

He sighed and shook his head, gesturing for her to come closer. Clara reluctantly obeyed, perching on his desk in front of him. Her arms still folded. He eyed the way her pink skirt pulled tight about her stomach and thighs. He ran his hands up the side of her leg grabbing her just below the hip. She finally smiled.

"When was the last time I fucked you?" he asked her.

"Yesterday" she immediately answered.

"Fuck is that all. It feels so long ago"

She leaned over placing her arms around his dark neck, noting the thickness of the greying goatee that adorned his face. "What's wrong Eddie?"

"Nothing. Just this case, I need the files"

She dotted little kisses on his lips "I will find it for you ok, don't worry"

"Fine" he conceded his mind now distracted. He slid a hand up the inside of her skirt, smirking as her legs parted in response. He delighted in the superiority she gave him.

"Unbutton your blouse" he demanded and without pause she complied, revealing the fullness of her bra. The phone on his desk rang. Clara leaned back to answer it.

"Dr Maxwell's Office. Oh hello… "

Edward slipped his hands into the bra releasing each breast in turn as she listened. He sucked one of her bare nipples into his warm mouth, the hairs on his face brushing against her soft skin. She gasped quietly "No I'm afraid he's unavailable at the moment…" she looked down into his eyes now burning with excitement and desire "He's with a patient. Can I take a message?…" Clara placed her hand over the receiver "Don't stop" she whispered, giggling. He reached up beneath her skirt, clutching at the top of her knickers and yanked them all the way down. Standing he shoved her legs wide apart "Sure yes ok, I will tell him..." she continued as he unbuttoned his trousers "Yes, yes of course..." he released himself and she grinned at the sight of his potent erection. He lifted her leg. Took hold of her from underneath and pushed himself inside her. "Ok thank you. Have a nice day" she managed before dropping the phone and groaning. Arching her back he drove himself in and out of her. She leaned up to kiss him, her tongue frantically exploring his mouth, his hand snatching at her breast. "I'm fucking you, I'm fucking you hard" he bragged. She writhed beneath him parting her thighs as far as she could allowing him to thrust deeper, "Yes you are" she moaned "Keep fucking me" his motion gained speed "Harder" she cried. The impact of his dick hurt her. She let out a small whimper. He kept pumping "I'm gonna come" he grunted holding tight on to her hips pulling her down on him "I'm gonna come up you" he repeated "Yes! Please, I want it, I want you" she breathed. "Fuck, Clara" he called out as finally his body shuddered and he poured inside her. She wrapped her arms around his large frame as he flopped on top of her. She stroked his sweaty bald head. The phone hung limply over the desk, a small yet detectable dialling tone. With him still throbbing inside her she spoke "Your wife called"

She slowly attempted to open her heavy eyelids, but they fell back down unable to sustain their own weight. There are strained voices in the distance, muffled, like they are spoken under water but her brain cannot connect to any word, they slip away from her like the waves of the sea. Her mind is once again consumed by unconsciousness.

"Sarah honey" the whisper finally drags her from the depths of her slumber. "Hmmmm?" she moans stretching out, her eyes still firmly shut. She felt a soft kiss on her neck. "Sarah" he spoke again. She blinked awake to find his smiling face close to hers, he leans in to kiss her. Images of the night before drove through her mind. She blushed.

"Oh hi" her voice is croaky.

"I have to be somewhere today" he strokes her hair as he continues "Do you want to come?"

"Where?" she asked her interest piqued.

"Back to Manchester, I have a meeting, and then I thought we could pick up Eric together?"

She sat up. A trip back there would give her chance to see Ariel.

"Yes definitely". His brow creased and he smiled uncertainly at her enthusiasm.

"I want to spend the day with you" she beamed rubbing her hand over his shoulder and praying she had extinguished his intrigue.

"Ok great. You get a shower and I will cook you, Mrs Ryan, some breakfast" he kissed her head and throwing on a t shirt and joggers, left the room. She caught the jacket out of the corner of her eye and wondered. Creeping out of the bed she patted it down. Empty. It was no use anyway, it was locked and she didn't know the passcode. *Dates.* Today she must uncover all special dates. Making a mental note she padded to his bathroom and flicking on the shower she slipped her already naked body under the warm running water.

It wasn't Ariel but a young gothic looking boy that brought Sarah her coffee. "Are you sure you will be ok here for a while?"
"John. I was fine last time. Go. Have your meeting, I have a book" she reassured
"Ok, ok. I'm going" he chuckled, kissing her and giving the hand he held one last squeeze he left the café, glancing back a few times to his waving wife. Once she watched him round the corner she called over the boy.
"Hey. Is Ariel here?" she whispered.
"Who wants to know?"
"Just a friend" Sarah offered,
"She's bobbed out to get some equipment, she's rewiring the cameras, I'll tell her you want her when she's back"
"Fine, thanks" Sarah slouched and the boy slunk away.
Ariel appeared about an hour later, her usual dishevelled self, although this time she had managed to wrestle her hair into a ponytail. The bottom half of her hair was shaved.
"Hey" Ariel started, her eyes darting round the coffee shop ensuring Sarah was alone.
"He's not here" Sarah offered "How you getting on?"
Ariel wiped her hand on her apron and sat down "Good, getting there. I have some stuff already but not everything, it's only been five days, I told you it could take a few weeks"
"I know, I know" Sarah whispered "but he was coming here today and I thought I would take the opportunity to see you"
"Well nice as that is lady I don't have your phone with me"
"Can you not call me lady" Sarah rolled her eyes "what can you tell me?"
"Well *Sarah*" she enunciated "I can't remember much, I didn't look through it but there's a lot coming through"
"Like what?" Sarah sat upright.
"Messages, emails, although they were a bit trickier, I had to hack your account"
"You hacked my account?" Sarah protested,
"How the fuck you think I do this lady...sorry SARAH"
"Fine, and..." she gestured for her to go on,

"Yea so messages, emails, call logs. I even got your calendar via your outlook, you were a busy woman" Ariel whistled.

"Busy, doing what?"

"Well by the looks of it a bloke named Tom"

It was like a slap in the face and it made Sarah's head spin. A wave of nausea crashed over her. This didn't make any sense.

"Pretty kinky too…"

"Ok. Stop!" she held her hand up, the colour drained from Sarah's face.

"Jeez, don't shoot the messenger lady, I did warn you, hey here's your man, Tom" Ariel winked.

Sarah's eyes shot up spying John gliding confidently and quickly towards the café his mouth upturned into a broad smile. *Fuck.* "You gotta go" Sarah choked, "Ahhhh I see, not Tom. Gotcha" Ariel rose "I'll text you, if you are still sure you want to know?"

She could see John's hand on the glass door, pushing it open in slow motion. The elongated ring of the bell tearing through her ears, he smiled. Sarah looked up at Ariel waiting expectantly, she looked back at John striding over to her, his face dropped, she turned to Ariel and nodded.

"Hey, everything alright? Are you bothering my wife?" he demanded.

"No man, just asking if she wanted anything" Ariel backed off defensively and before disappearing through a door way she winked again at Sarah.

"What's happened?" He knelt down beside her "You look like you have seen a ghost"

Maybe I have she thought.

(Sat 15thnov)

He may hold the key. She rapped lightly on his door. "Come in". He was sitting in front of two large screens, still wearing his batman pyjama pants and a black t shirt even though it was early afternoon. She smiled at him, as best she could, the familiarity of his face still as unsettling as the first time she saw him.

"Oh hey mum" he said, his voice gruff, removing the headset he had been wearing. "Hey. I erm, wondered if you could help me with something?" she mumbled.

"Sure come on in" he placed the headset carefully over a monitor and swivelled in his chair to face her. Sarah closed the door behind her and took a seat on the edge of his unmade bed. This was the first time they had been alone together. Being this close she could see the threads of lightness that give the same depth to his deep brown eyes as they do her own.

"What's up?" he smiled at her.

"It's kind of embarrassing" Sarah looked down at the pocket diary clasped beneath her hands. His screens jumps into life and there is a burst of gunfire. "Sorry, just let me leave this game" he stabs at the keyboard until the screen goes black and he returns.

"I, well, I hoped you could help me with some dates".

"Dates?" he enquired.

"Yes, birthdays, anniversaries, anything you think I should know".

He senses her embarrassment "Oh of course" he mouths the realisation dawning on him.

"I'm sorry" Sarah started, knowing it must be difficult for him, his own mother (potentially) unaware of the day she gave birth to him, void of all the memories in between.

"No mum! Don't be silly. Let me help"

"I just don't want to miss anything, you know"

"Yeah mum its fine. So where to start?". She ponders for a moment.

"What about my birthday" she settled on.

"You are April thirtieth, Dad is twenty second of Nov, next Saturday actually" Eric grinned.

"Good job I checked" Sarah mentioned, "Macy?" she continued.

"Yea, Macy's birthday is September ninth and mine is a day later the tenth"

"Wow really?" Sarah looked up from penning them into the diary.

"Yea I know, weird hey" Eric laughed.

"Well what are the chances" Sarah smiled

"About one in three hundred and sixty five" Eric answered and they both giggled. "Do you happen to know our wedding anniversary?" She ventured.

"Yea mum of course, it's Christmas Eve. Easy to remember". Christmas Eve, Sarah thought "That must have been one hell of a party" she muttered.

"Erm I don't think so, it was just you and dad. You eloped to Italy. Although the parties since have be good, well the ones I have been too" he nodded as if remembering them. Sarah had been slowly getting used to this life. The house they lived in. The cars they drove. But she realised she was still living a lie. The pretence of them all manoeuvring cautiously around each other without really engaging.

"So anything else you can think of I should remember?" she smiled softly at her son.

"Not that I can think of" he scratched at the mass of dark curls "Nope. Best ask Macy though just in case" he grinned.

"Ok well if that's everything" She rose to her feet,

"Wait actually, I erm, wanted to ask you something. If you don't mind?" Eric leant forward and put his arm out to stop her. She sat back down and looked into his youthful face, seeing the colour pinch at his cheeks. "Erm. Well I wanted to know, what exactly you remember?"

Her heart sank.

"Not much" she muttered, "Nothing really"

He leant back in his chair "Nothing at all?" he pushed.

"Well. No. I don't remember your dad, or Macy or you, I'm sorry" she couldn't look at him.

"Do you remember anything else?" he asked matter of factly and the directness of his question caused a washing of unease over Sarah. She cleared her throat. "Maybe" was all she could say.

"Mum" Eric started "I think you should know something, about before"

Sarah's heart drummed. It was becoming a regular thing. She wasn't sure if she wanted to hear this or flee from this moment. His eyes prickled. He wasn't sure how to do this, all of a sudden the words wouldn't come. His throat seized. Macy had made him promise. There was a knock at the door, it edged open. Instantly they both looked up.

"Hey I was looking for you" John announced "What are you guys doing in here?"

"Oh nothing" Sarah stuttered.

"We were just, erm, well it's a secret actually" Eric gleamed at his father.

"Really a secret?" he enquired entering Eric's bedroom. Sarah peered at their son inquisitively.

"Well next weekend is your birthday" Eric answered and Johns face lit up in amusement.

"Ah well if I can borrow your fellow conspirator?"

"Actually could you give us a moment? I'll be down in a minute?" Sarah stalled, "Doesn't matter Mum, we are done here anyway" and with that Eric turned, placed the headset over his ears and fired up his computer again.

"But it's Saturday?" Sarah enquired

"I know! I know! This is not an unusual occurrence believe me. I wouldn't ask but I really do need to head into the office. Could you, please?"

"Yes, yes of course. No problem" Sarah gulped. A whole afternoon. Just her and the children. "I won't be long" John lied knowing that this wouldn't be easy, let alone fast, but he had to end it now.

He kissed her briefly and jumped into the car. He knew he was leaving her little choice, but what could he do. He reversed out of the garage and headed off down the drive at speed. Waiting for the gate to open he picked up his mobile. Five missed calls and three text messages. He slammed the phone down and hit the gas. Directly across the road she was unmistakeable. Even with large dark sunglasses on against the autumnal sunshine the billow of red curls behind her gave her instantly away. *Fuck.* She remained motionless. Even though her eyes were hidden he could feel them boring into him. He didn't stop. He turned right, out onto the street and in his rear view mirror he watched her watching him speed away.

There was only one other car in the carpark as he flung it into his space. He bumped the sign that read his name with the grill of his Range Rover. *Shit fuck.* He fumbled with the door, jumping out and slamming it shut. He could only deal with one thing at a time. Gabrielle could wait.

Striding up to the entrance he could see her through the glass. Her eyes narrowed as he entered the atrium

"Glad you could make it" she smirked

"I didn't have much fucking choice now did I? You have to stop this Mabel right now. You can't keep calling and calling me."

"Drink?" she asked sashaying through the reception and into the kitchen at the back. He followed fury rising .

"Drink? No I don't want a fucking drink. I want you to leave me and my family alone" he spat, his fist clenched at his side. She rounded on him.

"Listen to me, and listen well. I will not leave you alone. Not until you leave her". Then he shoved her, driving her into the wall with force. Her eyes widened in shock. He slammed his forearm up against her neck which pushed her face away from him. Quietly he whispered in her ear

"Pack your things and leave, we are done here. You no longer work for me, and I want you to stay away from us all. Understand?" Mabel tried to wiggle free, but his grip on her was steadfast and his arm was starting to constrict her breathing. There was no point screaming, they were alone. "You know who I am and what I am capable of, so don't try me. Whatever we had is done, the promise is over. Leave now and you won't get hurt, I and all my resources won't come after you. But try me Mabel, and I promise you will regret it. Do not contact Sarah, do not even think about telling her"

A small tear appeared in the corner of her eye. His pumping blood slowed at the sight of it. He eased off letting her fall. Her hands flew to her neck as she took in a deep breath. Looking up at him she muttered,

"I don't believe you. I can't believe you are choosing her"

John crouched down to her level and harshly grabbed her chin. She tried to pull away. "Never underestimate what I would do to protect my family Mabel"

Chapter 13

The intercom rang, Eric clicked onto the driveway camera via the computer he was still sitting in front of. His stomach dropped. He threw down his headset and ran the length of the corridor skidding to a stop before the phone on the wall.

"Yes" he panted,

"I want to speak to Ava" the woman's voice demanded.

"Who are you?" Eric whispered.

"I want to speak to Ava" she repeated.

"There is no Ava here, what do you want?" he snapped.

"Who are you?" She asked.

"Me? Who the hell are you? I saw you. I saw you at my grandparents. I saw you here a few weeks back. What do you want?"

"Ava" was all she answered.

"There is no Ava here" he spat through gritted teeth.

"Well then tell John I was here. Looking for him"

Eric's mind raced. "What do you want with my dad?"

"Well that's an interesting question. Just tell him I was here" and she hung up. Eric replaced the phone and stared at it for a while. He needed to speak to Macy. Now.

"Hey everything ok?" Sarah appeared on the stairs "Who was it?" she nodded to the intercom.

"Oh no one, erm, salesmen that's all" he mustered a smile.

Her face creased "Ok, you sure?"

"Yea" Eric answered before heading back to his room.

"I have to pick up Macy, want to come with me?" Sarah yelled after him, "Actually yeah, just let me get changed" he threw back, pulling of his T-Shirt with his sweaty palms. He didn't want to stay here alone, with her outside, and he didn't want his mother to leave with the possibility of running into this woman. Eric didn't know for sure what she wanted but he sensed it wasn't good, and who was this Ava? He dressed quickly and ran down to the car. As soon as they pulled out his heart began to race. He had never noticed just how long their driveway was until now. Waiting patiently for the gate, Sarah looked across to Eric gazing out of the car window.

"You sure you are ok?" she asked for the seventeenth time. Something had spooked him, she knew that much.

"Yeah" he mumbled. As the street came into view Eric saw the Silver BMW parked across the street. He spotted the unmistakeable flash of red. His eyes darted to Sarah who obliviously looked through the traffic for a moment to safely pull out. The woman stood up from where she had been perched on her bonnet. Her eyes met his as she pulled off her sunglasses. She looked from Eric to his mother and her mouth fell open. He saw her form the word Ava as Sarah pulled out into the traffic and flicked on the radio. Through the wing mirror Eric could see her jumping and waving, but whatever she was screaming had been drowned out.

"Hey Eric, you know earlier today, in your room?" Sarah ventured, he made some noise in acknowledgement "Well, did you have something you wanted to tell me?" He saw the woman vanish behind them before answering.

"No not at all" and he turned up the music.

John climbed back in his car. He knew he had done enough to not expect her there on Monday morning. He punched out a message to Sarah checking if she had got Macy ok and placed his phone in the holder. It hadn't taken as long as he expected, Mabel was dealt with, quickly and quietly. He sighed as he looked at himself in the rear view mirror. He looked tired. His blue eyes surrounded by little jagged red capillaries, cutting random paths across the white of his eyeballs. His mobile shrilled. Sarah.

"Hi Honey" he mustered fake enthusiasm.

"Hi, I'm just on the way to get Macy now. Eric has come with me"

That lifted John's spirits. "Great. Well I won't be much longer I don't think. Just a few other things to sort out" he answered.

"Ok well, Eric and I had been talking and he mentioned that we used to go out on a Saturday night as a family. I wondered if you would be back in time for us to maybe do that?" Sarah ventured. He could hear the nervousness to her voice. "Sound's great. I'll make sure I'm home"

"Ok great" Sarah repeated "See you at home" and he clicked off.

John Ryan sat in his expensive car, outside the large offices of the company he owned and sighed. He was getting sick of feeling this way. He wanted control back. He knew what that entailed and so he slipped the car in to drive and once again sped away.

She was still there. He spotted the Silver BMW from a distance. As he got closer he slowed and while passing he made the gesture for her to follow him. She understood for immediately she hopped in the car and soon was tailing him, closer than was comfortable. Pulling into the fast food restaurant he parked far from the building in the empty back corner of the carpark. She quietly pulled up next to him and switched of the engine. He didn't look at her, he stared at the steering wheel for a moment before tugging on the handle and delivering himself to the setting sun.

"What the fuck is going on?" Gabrielle screamed even before he saw her fly round his car,

"Gabrielle please" John put his hands up defensively, but she struck him on the side of his face. It didn't move him, she had no real strength but it moved the anger inside him, dislodged it, sending it burning up inside him. For the second time today he clenched his fists.

"I don't see you for months, fucking months. You disappear and then this!" she continues to scream.

"Please Gabrielle stop" he grabbed her by the arm and dragged her round to the passenger side,

"Ouch John, get off me" she cried out.

"Shut the fuck up Gabrielle and get in the car". He bundled her into the seat and slammed shut the door. *Fucking women.* He climbed in his side, his piercing stare silencing her only momentarily

"What the fuck is going on?" she spat. He sighed again, shifting in his seat. Gabrielle's eyes narrowed and she started to laugh. It made him uncomfortable.

"What are you laughing at?" John snapped but she just continued to howl.

"Seriously Gabrielle, what's funny?" but when she ignored him again his temper finally won. Grabbing her by hair he yanked her face close to his. Her laughing ceased. Looking straight into his eyes she whispered "I saw her".

"A new man? That's great news! Who is it?" Ava asked

"His name is John England and he's gorgeous!" Gabrielle pulled the blanket they were sharing further up and took a glug of red wine. They spent most Saturday nights together when Tom was working, choosing to stay at Ava's small flat gossiping and ordering pizza "I've been dying to tell you!"

Ava sat up "Tell me more!" she smirked.

"Well he's hot, obviously, athletic and tall with blonde hair and the sexiest green eyes. He's sweet, and generous and...."

"...And?" Ava encouraged.

"Amazing at fucking me!" Gabrielle laughed.

"Gabrielle!"Ava gasped "You are so naughty" she smiled

"Oh Ava, not as naughty as him, I mean, some of the things..."

"Really what things? Tell me, leave no detail out" Ava grinned topping up her glass with water and pausing the film on the TV,

"He's got this deliciously thick, large cock..." Gabrielle regaled whilst Ava laughed. "Got any pictures?" Ava asked.

"Ava Adams!"

"I meant pictures of him, his face, not his, you know" she howled.

"Actually no" Gabrielle answered before adding "He's not keen on having his photo taken...."

"Oh god, not married is he?" Ava giggled, but Gabrielle just stared at her.

"Mum!" Eric almost shouted. "Huh? What?" She answered him. "You gonna go and knock or shall I?"

"Knock?" Sarah started.

"Forget it, you're miles away" Eric climbed out of the car leaving Sarah to sit with her memory. She tried desperately to fall back into it, there was something important to this one she knew, but just couldn't quite grasp what it was. The door behind her opened and Macy jumped in.

"Hi mum" she greeted her, Sarah mumbled something back.

"Who's that?" Sarah asked referring to the gothic looking girl waving in the driveway. "That's Leah mum, my best friend. Don't you remember she was round the day we flew to Malta?" Sarah focussed in on the young girl.

"Oh yes. Silly me" she waved back and once Eric was safely buckled in reversed away, the gothic girl still standing waving in her drive.

"We're going out tonight like old times" Eric smiled at his sister.

"Really?" Macy asked looking to her mother.

"Hmm. Yes going out" Sarah confirmed her mind still rolling round the memory.

"Awesome" Macy said "Some normality"

John had looked dishevelled earlier this evening when he had walked through the front door, but he had managed to paint a smile on his face up till now. Including throughout the nine turns of bowling, even if he hadn't yet won. Eric was hot on his heels and the final turn offered the chance of three bowls, if you were lucky enough. It wasn't luck, John knew, it was practice. The clatter of pins as the balls ploughed into them every few seconds filled the busy bowling alley. The haunting sweetness of the churning popcorn machine thickened the noisy air. Families laughing together, friends on a night out, a couple next to them, clearly on a first date. John watched as the tall youngster picked the girl up with surprising ease, her denim skirt revealing a tantalising glimpse of the curve of the underside of her bottom as he swung her round in celebration of a strike. John smirked.

"Dad" Eric shouted over the noise "You're up". Heaving himself up John grabbed his trusty green sixteen ball.

"Prepared to be destroyed" he cackled, poised, eyeing up the pins ahead, he lithely threw an expert ball, crashing through everything, sending all the pins hurtling into the back.

"Whoop! Strike" John punched the air.

"Well done honey" Sarah clapped. Eric moaned as his father, laughing, took him into a headlock.

"Still my go son" John winked at Sarah as he said it. Once it was all reset, he stepped up. Sarah couldn't help but notice the thickness of John's arms as he held the ball up to his chin. The tightness of his dark navy jeans against his thighs, the firm roundness of his bottom. He threw a confident look back to her, before throwing yet another strike. Eric groaned "For god sake!"

"Don't worry bro, you will win one day" Macy laughed.

"Boom!" John pointed triumphantly "That's a third go to me".

"Do you always get what you want?" Sarah asked quietly as he leaned down to steal a victor's kiss.

"Usually" he grinned. Even after his awful day, he was finally enjoying himself. He made this choice a long time ago, he was going to remain in control.

"I don't wanna finish now, can we go I'm starving" Eric whined facing certain defeat. John folded his arms.

"The Ryan's are not quitters Eric boy. You finish even when you think you don't have a shot at winning. You never know what's going to happen". Macy looked up from where she was sitting to smile at her father. "What?" John asked her. "Nothing" she shook her head with a small laugh.

"No go on, what?" John grinned. "It's just, well, Grampa just came out of your mouth". John looked to Sarah his faced dropped

"Shit. Quick let's get out of here" and they all laughed.

A gust of wind blew in, particles of rain slashed at their faces as John fought to push open the door into the violent dark night.

"Wait here I will go for the car" he shouted as he dashed outside, the door springing back in his wake. Sarah, Macy and Eric stood in the foyer of the bowling alley, the hammer of rain loud against the glass in which the three of them were now faced with their own reflections.

"Wow, the weathers turned" Eric offered.

"We can see that bro!" Macy laughed, her shaking head, engrossed in her phone. That reminded Sarah. Another gust of wet leaves flew in as a man held open the door to shout

"Help! Someone call an ambulance!"

Macy's head shot up from her phone. Eric looked to Sarah.

"What's happened?" a young girl with pink hair and facial piercing shouted back over the noise of blasted pins, wind and rain.

"Some bloke's been hit by a car"

The girl grabbed the receiver, Sarah's heart drummed.

"Stay here kids". She tightened the ties of her coat, pulling up her hood, head bent, she ran out into the dark car park. There he was, and for a moment all breath left her. He lay out on the wet floor, face down in a puddle that reflected the neon sign above.

"Hey love, do you know this man?" the guy behind her asked.

"Yes, he's my husband" Sarah answered meekly. A few people started to gather, but Sarah was frozen.

"Here come help me" the man shouted over as he slid to his knees in front of an unconscious John. Sarah hobbled over unsteadily. She looked back to the Bowling Alley, she could see Macy and Eric clearly, the brightness making it appear like a video playing on a black wall.

"Please somebody take the children inside" Sarah shouted and a lady with a wisp of a grey hair that had escaped her hat and was now whipping her weather beaten face, nodded in acceptance, and dashed inside. Sarah dropped to the floor beside John.

"He's breathing" the man said "I'm a vet, not quite the same but I'm all you got". Sarah nodded.

"Can you support his neck?" John was sprawled at such and angle it looked like his neck had snapped.

"How?" she mumbled.

"Your coat. Take off your coat, roll it up" the vet shouted to her as he checked Johns pulse and pulled open his eyes. She did as she was told, and only when she slid the coat as instructed as gently as possible under him did she realise the puddle in which john lay had stained her jeans, red.

Chapter 14

He felt her shaking him before his ears picked up on the sound. He clambered to answer the call and managed to mumble a sleepy "Hello" as he rubbed open his eyes and checked the clock on his matching mirrored bedside table. 2:43am. The delivery of the news was quick and efficient but that was Clara for you. He slammed down the receiver, flicked on the lamp and started to dress.
"What's wrong?" she blinked against the sudden light invasion.
"It's a patient, go back to sleep Adele". Tucking in his shirt, he grabbed the car keys from where he kept them, safely in the top drawer, threw on his jacket and headed out the room. Almost running down his grand Victorian stair case his wife appeared after him pausing at the top, tying her lilac satin rob around her waist. "Wait, Edward, when will you be back?"
"Late".
"Again? But the boys have their recital this afternoon".
Edward paused momentarily to think.
"What time?" he glanced back at her.
"Two"
He rushed to open the large brass lock and answered "I'll be there" before slamming shut the heavy front door. The noise made her jump. She looked around their grand, now quiet home, the black and white family photos of them that adorned the cream walls. Deciding to get a coffee considering she was already awake, Adele hoped with all her might that he would make it to the recital, for the sake of their boys. He wouldn't miss another one, would he?

"Dr Maxwell" he boomed, his badge held high as he stormed the A&E department. "Where is my patient? Where is Mr Ryan?"
Holding on to the edge of the reception desk his knuckles turned white.
"Who are you?" the woman enquired.
"I'm his doctor and I'm here to move him to my private hospital"
The woman typed frantically, "Nope sorry"
"Nope sorry?" he repeated "Do you know who this patient is for god sake? He's being moved. Now!"
She popped her chewing gum "You'll have a hard time, doctor, he's in surgery. His wife is down the hall in the family room" she pointed a long sinewy finger.
"Get me the admitting doctor asap. And stop chewing gum in here." he shouted heading in the direction she gestured, his coat billowing out behind him. A couple of knocks on the door he heard her feeble voice. Sarah was dishevelled. She had clearing been soaking wet at some point, her blood shot eyes screamed fatigued. "Good god Sarah, are you ok?" he slipped in to the seat beside her, she recoiled from him.

"Oh I'm so sorry I didn't wish to alarm you, I'm the family doctor, Dr. Edward Maxwell".

He saw her exhale "Oh yes, I remember".

"You do?" he gasped, noticing the slight elevation in his own heartbeat.

"Yes, you were there at the hospital when I woke up". His heart rate slowed.

"Oh yes that's right, after your, accident. I'm here now to take you and Mr Ryan to our hospital"

Sarah pushed her matted hair out of her face "You can't, he's in surgery, I don't know how long he will be or actually what's even happening." She swivelled the contents of her cold plastic cup.

"Right leave this to me I will get an update, and you a fresh cup of coffee, and me one for that matter. Wait right here Sarah, erm, Mrs Ryan"

He laboured to stand but before he could grab the handle the door opened and a doctor in his scrubs entered pulling the blue hat from his head.

"Mrs Ryan, your husband is out of surgery, he had a dislocated shoulder, which we managed to reset. There was some internal bleeding which we have controlled, and he appears to have a few cracked ribs. He will need to be admitted for monitoring, as there could have been a brain injury. But for now he's stable I would like to get an MRI scan"

Edward put his hand up "I'm Dr Maxwell, I'm Mr Ryan's doctor, I want him moved to my hospital asap"

There was an immediate tension between the two men, the other doctor spoke to Sarah "Mrs Ryan I wouldn't advise moving him right now"

Edward looked at her and interrupted "Sarah, let me assess John and if he is stable enough to move he would be better off at my hospital. You pay for the very best medical care, let me assure you. This is what he would want" the small nod she gave him was all he needed. Both doctors left and she was once again alone with her turmoil.

Edward guided her to his Mercedes some time later. It was a risk he knew it but he couldn't just deliver her home, confused and alone in an empty house.

"So how about we pick you up some clean clothes and you can come back to my house where Adele will look after you?"

Her eyes widened "Your House? Adele?"

Opening the car door he tried to dissipate her concern "You used to be friends, you and Adele. She will help you"

Sarah looked up at him through the window as he gently closed the door behind her and clambered around to his side.

"Friends?" she ventured.

He nodded in response. "Close friends, at one time" he slipped the car into reverse and drove out of the carpark and away from the hospital, a private ambulance ahead. Sarah turned the word around in her mind 'Friends' as she turned from him to watch the blurring dance of the city lights through the rain as they sped away.

Adele was dozing, she hadn't returned to a restless sleep, so when the door clicked open she sat up. The clock read 5:38am. She flung off the duvet and slipped her feet into the matching lilac slippers, she was throwing on her robe when she heard them. Two voices. She strained, slowing her actions for a moment to listen. Was it really her? She crept out, catching a glimpse of them before they disappeared down the hallway, it was. Adele took the stairs quietly trying to catch their conversation but she crashed into her husband as he walked back out of the kitchen.
"Hey" she pushed her hair back, he looked down at her and raised an eyebrow.
"I was just looking for you" she whispered "I heard you come in, you have company!"
He pulled her to one side and lowered his voice even more, "It's Sarah. The patient this morning, it was John, he's been in an accident. She's still confused and doesn't remember anything so I thought it best, you know..."
"She still doesn't remember?" Adele choked.
"No! So be careful what you say"
She nodded.
"I have to get back to the hospital. Can you look after her?"
"Of course, of course. Go" He leant in to kiss her before running out the door.
Adele walked into her kitchen. Sarah was sat at the breakfast bar. She turned at the sound but there was no recognition that flashed across her face, no friendly smile to greet her. Adele swallowed hard and mustered a smile.
"Hi, I'm Adele, Edwards wife" Sarah shook her extended hand
"Sarah"
"Let me get you a drink" Adele whirred the industrial looking coffee machine into action and expertly pulled on the levers "Coffee?" Sarah nodded in response.
"So how is John?" Adele asked. The sad woman in front of her rubbed at her head before answering.
"I don't really know yet. Dr Max...your husband is having him assessed at his hospital. I didn't even get to see him"
Adele leaned over to take her hand "He's in the best hands"
"I'm sure" Sarah smiled meekly.
"Where are the children?" Adele asked as she retrieved some cups from a top cream cupboard.
"Oh with John's parents, Macy called them, apparently I don't have any so..."
Adele ignored the statement, she wanted to steer away from the past as much as possible.
"How are they?"

"Worried, hysterical, afraid. This must be hell for them. Both parents in accidents within a few weeks of each other" Sarah's eyes started to glisten, and as Adele rested a comforting hand on hers the tears began to flow. Adele flew round to Sarah's side and the women embraced. She held her friend as she sobbed, the past didn't matter right now. What mattered was this confused version of her once closest ally and the children Adele had watched grow, they needed her.

"Everything will be ok. Edward will fix John and I will fix us coffee, and after that I will show you to a guest bedroom and you can rest" she smiled at her.

"Thank you so much, sorry to be a burden"

"Not at all. Edward will know where to find you then when he has news"
Sarah welcomed the warm mug Adele had offered

"Thanks. I best call Macy and Eric, let them know what's happening"

"Good idea, let me show you upstairs and you can have some privacy"
Sarah gratefully followed the familiar stranger. She thanked her for the fluffy baby blue pyjamas Adele laid out for her and once alone Sarah lay back heavily on the bed and sobbed. The only anchor she had in this mass of confusion was lying in a hospital bed. Sarah had no idea what to do. She took the phone out of her bag and dialled Macy's number. She gave her as much information as she had and as much reassurance as she could deliver, the last thing Sarah wanted was the guilt that the children were worried. There was no denying the fondness that she had developed for them. It was then she remembered. The hospital had given them too her, John's possessions.

His wallet and his phone.

She scrambled to find it at the bottom of her bag, but her diary, she knew exactly where that was, in the top drawer of her bedside cabinet. *Shit.* Swiping it into life she fought desperately to retrieve the dates Eric had given her. John's birthday, that was Saturday, he would be forty six, her brain screamed against the cloud of numbers counting back on her fingers. Nineteen seventy. Her fingers found 161170. Nothing. *Think Sarah.* September she knew that, but the number rushed before her. Ninth maybe. Worth a shot. 0909. Wait what year? once again she counted back, twice to double check, two thousand and one. 01. Nothing. Was the ninth Eric's or Macy's birthday? She tried again this time figuring out Macy's year of birth. Nineteen ninety nine.

 090999. Nothing
100901. Nothing
100999. Nothing.

Sarah became aware that she only had so many chances at this, and then the phone would wipe, or delete, or spontaneously combust or something. Her foot drummed against the floor. What other dates. Ah, the easiest one to remember, Christmas Eve, their wedding anniversary. What year? Did he say they were married seventeen years, or eighteen, or was it twenty? Sarah cursed her memory. For more than the current difficulties she was suffering.

241298. Nothing
241297. Nothing
Three attempts remaining. *Fuck.*
241296. Nothing
Two attempts remaining. *Fuckety Fuck.*
Her own birthday! But she couldn't remember, April possibly. She had one chance left, Sarah couldn't risk the last attempt and blocking the phone, or a fireball in this pristine bedroom. She took a deep breath and carefully typed 300477. The screen sprung into life.

Chapter 15

The hum of machinery woke him. He squinted against the dim light as pain seared through his chest. He tried to speak but the dryness of his mouth made it impossible. Plus any movement caused a fresh slice of fiery agony to tear through his lungs. John's fingers clasped round something, it felt smooth in his hand. He pressed the button on the top and was relieved to hear the buzzer. He recognised Edward immediately.

"John, you're awake. Don't try to move too much, you're in pretty bad shape but we have you now, you are in the best place. You were knocked over outside a bowling alley"

The memory came flooding back. He had beaten Eric. He left for the car. The rain pelted his face.

"How's the pain from one to ten?"

John released all his fingers without lifting his arms.

"Ok" Edward said "I'm going to administer some morphine. You may get drowsy. We are going to sedate you for a head CT. Don't worry though Sarah is at home with Adele"

John's eyes widened "No" he croaked, wincing against the pain.

"It's ok John. She won't say anything" the doctor whispered and he relaxed back allowing the drugs to wash over him and drag him down into the pain free slumber.

"Everything is normal" Edward told Sarah over the phone "He's got a small crack in a rib, a reset shoulder but other than that his scans were clear. You can come in anytime to visit, but I suggest you get some rest first"

She had accepted his advice and he rang off feeling slightly more confident, but only slightly. He hoped that Adele would keep her promise to him. Looking up he spotted her striding down the corridor a holder with two Starbuck's cups in, she smiled broadly.

"I brought you this, thought you would need it"

"Thanks" he muttered taking the cup and returning his phone to his pocket.

"How is he?" she enquired.

"Not too bad luckily"

Clara nodded "I closed your surgery for today and rescheduled your appointments, some of them I pushed to the local GP's"

Edward nodded his appreciation.

"Anything else you want me to do?" She asked.

"No. Just stay here. In case I need you"

"Ok. I can do that"

"Oh, and ensure I get to the boys recitals at two today"

"Ok. I can do that too"

"Good. Because if I miss that I'm in more trouble than I ever been and I need her onside at the moment"

The "her" needed no introduction, Clara knew it meant Adele and she rarely spoke her name. Adele and her knowledge, whatever that was, was what kept Clara from her happily ever after.

"Well you always need her onside, for some reason" she mumbled.

"We talked about this Clara…"

"I know" she held her hand up defensively "But I still think you're stupid. Whatever it is we could get through together…"

"Please not here" he dragged her into a private room away from the nurse's station slamming the door shut he started "Clara I told you I can't leave, this is it. This is all I will ever have to offer you, that's never going to change"

"Why?" She demanded throwing her bag down on the table and slinking into a chair.

"Fucking hell. Really? Right now? We are doing this again right fucking now, when I have John Ryan lying in a bed a few doors away?" he snapped. Her face fell. He was intimidating enough, a man of his height and stature, but he had a voice that filled even the vastest of rooms. She needed to back pedal and fast.

"Sorry, I'm sorry" she rose, running her hands up his chest and over his shoulders. He initially turned from her and her face had to follow his to kiss him. She slipped her tongue into his mouth and when he finally returned her passion she slid a hand down the front of his trouser and rubbed at the growing member beneath the fabric.

"I could cheer you up?" she smiled pulling away from him "Right here in this room, I could cheer you up?" she licked at her top lip suggestively and kissed him again.

"Stop" he gently held her away from him.

"Stop what?" she enquired naughtily, her brows pulling together in mock confusion. She slipped her top over her head and let it fall to the floor. She was wearing no underwear.

"Fuck it" He slammed her up against the wall and she laughed with anticipation.

John pressed the button frantically. A nurse entered and just as quickly retreated at his demand for Dr Maxwell. Her plastic shoes squeaked against the vinyl floor as she hurried to locate him, she witnessed his escape into the small room with his secretary and she guessed he may not welcome the interruption. Alas there was no choice, she lightly tapped on the door ignoring the tell-tale noises.

"Dr. Maxwell, Mr Ryan is awake and demanding to see you" she spoke through the door as silence fell inside the room. He coughed and mumbled some answer before a few moments of scuttled movement finished and he appeared. She had to look up to face him, a colour easily detectable in his dark cheeks.

She stepped back to allow him to stride past her and the woman still in the room adjusted her top and smiled brightly.

"John. I'm here, everything ok?" Edward started as he entered the private hospital room.

"Sit me up"

The bed rose smoothly at the press of a button. John winced but the drugs hadn't completely worn off so the pain was duller than he expected. It allowed him the reprieve needed to edge up the bed.

"Get Sarah here"

"John, Sarah is asleep at my house. She was pretty shook up, I think you should…"

"Get her here now Edward" he snapped, his eyes ablaze with determination. Edward had treated this patient, this friend, long enough to know when argument was feeble. He nodded and turned to leave.

"When can I go home?" John asked after him.

"It will be a few days yet, I need to monitor the internal…"

"Tonight" John stated, "Make it tonight"

"What?" Edward turned on him "I can't discharge you tonight, you've been hit by a car John. You need to be in here"

"You know why I have to get home Edward. Adele."

"Adele won't tell Sarah anything, I have already told you this, your secrets are safe"

"My secrets? How is Clara anyway? Still fucking her?" his eyes narrowed

"John…please, you need to stay for your health"

"I can risk that. I need to be home, Sarah needs to be home. Do what I pay you to do"

Edward cast his eyes down to the floor, his heart sank. He wasn't used to being pushed around, especially not by those he once cared for, and recently he felt he couldn't even look at the man in front of him. He knew that once again in the walls of his own hospital, his own empire, he was going to lose yet another battle to John Ryan.

Her stomach churned. The image of her father's lifeless body sprawled out wouldn't leave her mind. Sobs came silently, not wanting to draw attention to her room, a silly idea Macy thought, her grandparents' manor house was so vast she could probably scream and not be heard. Still she didn't want to risk it. She didn't want anyone in her space. Not even her brother, who she desperately wanted to comfort. Macy needed to process. How could this have happened? As if their family hadn't been through enough. The morning light began to seep through the gap in her heavy curtains, sleep had escaped her all night. The nausea she felt as she tried to move, wanting to pull the curtains too, eliminated Macys desire to shut away the day, she couldn't rest feeling so ill. Her head spun. She turned her back to the window, pulling the duvet over

her face and shut her eyes tight willing this feeling to pass. The call with her mother should have set her mind at rest, it did a little, but that wasn't what bothered her. There was a knock at the door. Without waiting for a response the door creaked open and she heard her grandmother whisper "Macy?"
She grunted.
"Oh Macy darling, how are you feeling? Have you heard from your mother?" Macy pulled the duvet back "Yes, Dad's ok. Broken rib and he dislocated his shoulder but he's ok. Stable"
Rita nodded. "Yes, Dr Maxwell called your grandfather" she perched on the edge of the four poster bed they had bought for Macy from Thailand a few years back. Their granddaughter had been obsessed with dolphins, the very animal that adorned the tops of the posts, ornately carved into the dark wood, they knew they had to purchase it. Macy had been so excited to sleep under the canopy supported by her favourite creatures. Rita recalled vaguely that Macy had named them, but shook off the memory, it held no importance when her only son had almost died.
"Do you know what happened exactly Macy?"
"What do you mean Grandma? He was hit by a car" her eyes stung.
"I'm sorry dear I don't want to upset you, but your grandfather, he wants answers. Did you see the car? Remember it? Maybe caught a glimpse of the driver?" Rita ventured. The sickness washed over her again. Her mouth filled with saliva and Macy had to gulp down against the violent need to gag.
"No" she lied "I didn't see anything" a lone tear ran down her cheek wetting the pillow
"Ok, ok" Rita patted her arm and leaned in to kiss her forehead "I'm sorry to ask, I will leave you to sleep" she rose, her floor length leopard print silk robe swelling out behind her "Get some rest" she added before pulling closed the door. Macy turned back toward the window, she focused on the dust particles dancing in the sun rays. Rest, if only she could. Memorising that registration meant not only had she seen the car, she knew exactly who had driven into her father, and it was no accident.

Chapter 16

Please leave her.
I will forgive you for going back x

Sarah had been staring at the text for at least ten minutes. It was the first one she had found, sent only last night, from the same person she had accidently answered in their bedroom. Mabel. It was an unusual name, could it be the same Mabel she had so fleetingly remembered on her date with John, her Mabel? What did it mean? *Leave her. Forgive you?* Sarah struggled. She clicked back, the other messages were from work, the children, his father. Nothing to give her any clues. She looked back at the one solitary message. Nothing before. Probably deleted. Sarah toyed with the idea of calling the number, asking Mabel, whoever she is, who exactly she wanted him to leave and what she would forgive her husband for. The anger rose in Sarah, it felt alien to actually feel something so violently. The blood pulsed through her neck, her finger hovered over the phone icon wanting desperately to press it and challenge this Mabel, who may or may not have once worked for her. Sarah clicked off it. She relented. Moving through the screens she opened his emails, Mabel, her again! As Sarah's eyes scanned the pages they were all work related, she noted the signature below the email, PA to the CEO. Her mind struggled to make any coherent sense of this, Mabel was now Johns PA? There were many emails, none of which seemed to hold any other content but a professional manner, an employee and her boss. The front door slammed closed outside. Sarah looked at the clock on the mantelpiece of the fireplace in the vast guest bedroom. 8AM. Adele must be leaving to take the young boys in the photos to school. She returned her attention to the emails. There was one from his father marked **Urgent- Delete** he obviously hadn't followed instructions. It was dated prior to her accident. Sarah opened it.

Jay

We were visited again last night. I paid the final instalment £500,000 needs to be put back into the company account. Make sure it's done. Quickly. Delete this.

John Ryan Snr
Chairman

Five hundred thousand pounds, Jesus. Scrolling through there was no other explanation or intriguing correspondence, some group email with Peter, Henry and Alexander alluding to a golf trip to Portugal. Plane tickets to Malta, Home

Insurance quote he had forwarded to Mabel. Great she now dealt with their household matters too! Sarah's blood boiled. Order confirmations for online shopping, a Tag watch, some clothes from Ralph Lauren, blar, blar, blar. Something in her mind twigged. It connected invisible dots. Malta. Frantically swiping the page down to the plane tickets email Sarah opened them up. Maria's story, when they were last there, the bruises, maybe there was a date to be found. She read quickly, the recent trip. Macy's tickets, Eric's, her's, Johns, and then nothing before 2014. She blinked at the screen. It seemed all their tickets going back years were in this folder but between 2014 and the trip they all recently took there was nothing, but she knew she had been there. The room started to swirl. This didn't make sense. Tiredness hit her like a freight train. She hadn't slept for more than twenty four hours and her brain hurt like hell. Clicking shut the phone, Sarah scrambled into the large bed, slipping her shoes off as she did. Without the energy to change the Pyjamas stayed where Adele had laid them. This was a mess, and she was too exhausted to begin to make sense of it all so Sarah closed her eyes and gave up.

"I'm going to see dad" Macy declared on entering lunch "Will you take me or shall I get a taxi?"
"I'm coming too" Eric said a mouth full of sandwich.
Their grandfather looked up from the large broadsheet he was reading and pulled off his glasses "Why would you get a taxi Macy?"
"Exactly" her grandmother added "David will drive you"
"David? Your driver?" Macy's huffed.
"You're not coming Grandfather?" Eric enquired his eyes wide.
"My boy, we own a prominent company, if the press see me entering a hospital they will get a whiff of a story, assume I'm dying at the very least and the shares will plummet" John Sr answered.
"Really grandad, shares? Mum has no memory, dads lying in a hospital and you're worried about fucking shares?"
"Macy!" Rita screamed, but no answer came. Silence hung in the air momentarily allowing John Snr's blood pressure to rise quietly. He shot up.
"How dare you, in my house" he boomed, striding over to a defiant looking Macy he struck her hard across her face, her legs buckled and she collapsed onto the pink dining room carpet.
"Grandad!" Eric yelled running to his sister, he dropped down to wrap her in his arms and they both turned their faces up to him. John Snr glared.
 "I will not tolerate language like that from you, do you hear? Now get out of my sight before I throw you out on your ear"
Before scrambling to her feet with the help of her brother, Macy took a moment to eye her grandfather. She looked from him to her grandmother quietly pouring some tea from the pot, her bracelets jangling from a slight, just

detectable, tremor. Eric stuck out his chin and held his sister steady as together they fled from the room.

"David?" Eric called as they both ran to the downstairs kitchen "Can you please take Macy and I to the hospital to see our father?"

David folded the paper and slammed it playfully on the long table that dominated the room.

"Sure" he smiled before noticing the redness appearing along Macy's cheek, his amusement slipped away "Come on I will take you both now" he grabbed his coat and kissed his wife, who happened to be the cook for the family and ushered them out of what would have been, and still was it seemed, the servants entrance.

The place was quiet, only the soft jazz music floating from the speakers filled the air. Tom was placing the final sprig of parsley on the pasta dish as he turned, a plate in each hand, a broad smile spread across his face. She sat bathed in the flickering light from the candles that adorned the neatly set table in her tiny flat.

"What is all this for Tom?" Ava smiled.

"I can't cook my beautiful girlfriend a meal without an agenda?"

He placed the dinner in front of her and the delicious aroma of tomatoes and garlic engulfed her.

"Wow, thank you. This looks amazing"

Tom reached over as he sat and took her hand in his.

"I want to say a prayer. Dear lord, thank you for the food you have blessed us with. Thank you for bringing Ava to me. Keep her safe during this pregnancy and deliver us of a healthy child. Amen"

"That was beautiful" she whispered patting her growing stomach lovingly.

He leant over and kissed her before sliding from his chair and on to one knee. From his pocket he produced a small, black velvet box. Ava gasped.

"Ava, this last year has been the greatest of my life. I love you. I love our unborn child, and I promise to look after you both…"

The phone sitting on the woven table in the hallway rang interrupting his speech, Tom's head dropped.

"Ignore it…please" she said

"Wait what if it's him again?"

"Who?" she snapped her eyes filled with desperate encouragement, don't stop now she thought. He rose, the box still clasp in his grip, strode over to the receiver and answered it. His face fell as a moment later he slammed it down and ran to the window.

"What? Tom what is it?" she felt her throat close as she fought to get the words out, she swallowed hard "Tom?"

He half turned his face to her, unable to make eye contact, "He apologised for interrupting my proposal" he spoke over his shoulder.

"What?" Ava gasped
"It's got worse Ava. Now he, whoever he is, is watching us"

Sarah gasped, shooting up right, the sweat was dripping down her back, she took a few deep breaths and tried to steady the tremble in her hands. She was pregnant. She and Tom were having a baby. There came a small knock at the door. Frantically she clambered up and opened it ever so slightly. Adele stood in the hallway a drink and a sandwich in hand.
"It's midday, I thought maybe you would be hungry" Adele smiled warmly.
"Oh right" Sarah patted at her hair and opened the door allowing Adele to enter. She laid the lunch down on the large mirrored dresser.
"How are you feeling?"
Sarah didn't hear the question at first, her mind was struggling to determine if this was in fact reality, having been in such a vivid dream so recently, she scanned the room to get her bearings and took a laboured seat on the bed. Adele repeated the question.
"Oh, Yes. Fine. Thanks" Sarah mumbled.
"You don't look fine" Adele responded sitting on the cream stool in front of the dresser "In fact you look really pale, should I call Edward?"
"No! Sorry, no thanks I am fine really, maybe I do need something to eat"
Adele passed her the plate and offered her a small smile of encouragement. Sarah took a bite, but contrary to easing her suffering it turned her stomach. She struggled to swallow it under the watchful eye of her host.
"Adele?" Sarah ventured once she was free of the piece of bread "Edward told me we used to be friends, what happened?"
Sarah saw the shock Adele tried so hard to hide, she spotted instantly the slight widening of the eyes, the way her lips fell open just marginally.
"Nothing, really, we are friends" Adele laughed a little.
"Really? Because I sense that something may have happened and I'm really struggling here. I am in a life I don't remember, I have a husband and two children I don't know, and I seem to have zero friends" Sarah sighed.
"Sarah..." Adele began,
"No, stop. I can't take another person pussy footing around me. I need help Adele, and if it's true, if we were ever friends then please help me" she pleaded.
Adele remained motionless, images of them laughing together on the many holidays they took flashed through her mind, the time they had to be carried out of the vineyard in San Francisco by their husbands after getting too carried away. The sleepovers when either Edward or John were working away, the night Sarah turned up soaking wet and bruised.
"We were friends. Best of friends" Adele began quietly "We used to always be together"
"What happened?"

"I don't know" Adele lied.

"Adele. Please" Sarah pleaded "If I was ever good to you, help me"

"Oh Sarah, you were the best! I wish you could remember all the years of friendship. We really were inseparable, you are god mother to my sons for goodness sake."

"I am?"

"Yes! I was bridesmaid at your wedding, I was the first visitor when you had Macy, and Eric, I was your best friend and you mine"

"Well what happened?"

"It's hard to explain. Do you remember anything?"

"Yes"

"Yes!" Adele exclaimed "What?"

"That I'm someone else altogether. That my name is Ava and I live in a small flat with my boyfriend Tom and we are going to have a baby"

Adele's face fell. Her heart quickened in her chest. She chewed her lip and looked away from her friend and out the window across her manicured lawn below.

"Adele, what is it?" Sarah questioned seeing the shift in her.

"I really think you should forget about Ava, or Tom or any baby, its seems like it could be confusion from the accident"

"But it's not" Sarah assured "It's real, the memories are so vivid and tangible I know they are real, I know I am Ava"

Adele turned on her "How can you be Ava when you are Sarah?" she asked.

"I, I don't know"

"Look around you Sarah, you have a wonderful husband, two beautiful children, let's just get on with life and forget all about Tom and Gabrielle and some imaginary baby. Eat lunch and maybe later we can go grab the children from Rita and John together ok" she patted Sarah's hand as she got up to leave.

"Adele wait"

Adele mustered the best smile she could as she turned back to face Sarah.

"I never mentioned anything about Gabrielle"

His mobile shrilled constantly in his pocket and he tapped his foot desperate to leave the room and answer it.

"Everyone in agreement then, with medical care at home we will discharge Mr Ryan"

The other five doctors around the boardroom table nodded and Edwards's shoulders relaxed. He could get John home and Sarah where she belonged, and the nagging worry of his wife relinquishing on her promise would be gone.

"Thank you gentlemen of the board" Edward offered before rushing from the room as discreetly as possibly. Once safely outside in the corridor he grabbed the phone from his pocket. Fifteen missed calls from Adele and one voicemail.

His face fell as he listened to it. Those two words made the walls sway and the floor beneath him shake "She knows".

"There you are, did you get them to agree?" Clara was walking towards him but he couldn't quite focus "Is the mighty John Ryan getting what he wants as usual?" she smirked but his vision warped. He lost his grip on the phone, hurtling to the floor with a smashing sound. Edward leant on the wall to stop himself from falling

"Edward honey, are you ok?" Clara held on to him as he feebly shook his head "Nurse! Nurse get over here I need some help, put him in that chair. Quickly" They both stumbled under the weight of him but managed to slide him down in the wheel chair, three other nurses rush over with machines as Clara is pushed out of the way. He brushes them off as they attempt to help

"Get away from me" he boomed, regaining his strength "My phone, where is my phone?"

Clara bent to retrieve it offering up the smashed face to him.

"Fuck! Clara your phone now" he demanded "Go away" he shouts to the nurse still unsurely lingering unconvinced of his recovery. He snatches the phone from Clara once she dug it out of her bag, rose and marched down the hallway to his office. Clara didn't follow. She knew well to leave him when a mood as dark as this descended. He slammed shut the door and turned the lock. Punching his home telephone number in he slumped into the large leather seat behind his desk.

"Hello"

"What do you mean she knows?" he spat through gritted teeth.

"I messed up, she was opening up to me about Tom and the baby, and I mentioned Gabrielle, I'm so sorry" Adele whispered frantically on the other end.

"Jesus Christ Adele she's only been there a few hours and you have managed to fuck up months of work"

"I know, I know I'm sorry" She cried.

"Don't start fucking crying now. You better fix this Adele. I mean it"

"I don't know how"

"Well what did you say, after you mentioned Gabrielle?"

"I told her I overheard John had mention her and Tom to you because he was worried"

"Did she buy it?"

"I don't think so..." she tailed off "I don't know what to do!"

"I'm on my way home soon, I will fix this. Try not to fuck anything else up" and he clicked off. Before he could go anywhere he needed to orchestrate John's transfer home and at least then Adele would be nowhere near Sarah. He opened up his computer and started to fill in the long list of forms.

Chapter 17

Walking up the corridor Macy made Eric promise not to tell their father about the strike she had received at the hands of their grandfather. He had promised against his better judgement but only because of the look of terror written on his sister's face. They were waiting for John to wake from a sleep, he had been deeply sleeping since they arrived over an hour ago, drug induced the nurse had said. Macy was absentmindedly flipping through a magazine not registering the images on the page. His snores faltered.

"Dad?" Eric jumped up. Johns eyes opened slowly, his pupils contracting to take in his surroundings, he had until a second previous been embroiled in a terrifying nightmare.

"Hey dad" Macy soothed "Its Macy and Eric, we have come to see you"

John coughed and winced, groaning against the searing pain in his chest. He slammed on the morphine pump Edward had placed into his hand earlier today and reclined awaiting the freedom the drug administered.

"Hi kids" he croaked.

"Hi, how are you feeling?" Macy enquired taking his hand. He gave it a reassuring squeeze. His face was swollen and dark blue around one eye, as he smiled a wound stretched against its meagre scab at the corner of his slightly enlarged lip, it still turned up into a smile.

"I've been better. How's mum? Have you spoken to her?" he whispered.

"Yes this morning, she is at Adele's. She seems shaken"

"Well can you imagine how this is for her, her accident and now this? She doesn't even know who she is. I'm worried about her"

"Dad, don't worry we will be home later and we will take care of her" Eric chimed with enthusiasm.

"Thanks kidda" John smiled at him, still holding tight onto his ribs.

"Eric will you do me a favour and go get me a cup of coffee?" Macy asked producing a fiver from her purse "And something for you"

Eric sighed "That's it, get rid of the youngest while you 'talk about things'. I'm in this family too you know"

"Eric, please. I promise I will tell you everything but first I just need to speak to dad about something" she pleaded.

"Fine" he submitted and sloped off.

"Hey what's going on?" John turned to his daughter the tension clear on her face.

"You know the accident" Macy began slowly.

"Mine or mums?" John laughed against the pain trying to ease whatever was worrying her.

"Yours" She gulped "I know who hit you"

John's eyes widened, he tried to sit up, but the morphine that was helping him fight against the pain was now dragging him into a sluggish mist. "What?" he gasped "Who?"
"The woman that came to the house, the one with the red hair" and with that John's heart rate on the monitor beeped into a speedy response.

Sarah returned the dishes to the kitchen, Adele wasn't there, which suited Sarah just fine. Ever since the message had come through on her phone Sarah had a new found purpose. People were lying to her, she could sense it, she may have hit her head in the accident but she wasn't stupid. She slipped the plate as quietly as she could into the sink and put her bag over her shoulder. Heading out into the hallway she heard Adele's footsteps above, she retreated back into the kitchen. There was no other option she would have to leave by the back door. She hurried back through, over to the french doors leading out to the garden. It was a miserable, overcast day with the threat of a storm. The kind of day that encouraged people to stay inside but right now all Sarah wanted was to escape and she couldn't trust that Adele would let her. She pushed on the handles but they didn't budge. Keys. She felt along the shelves on the wall. No keys. She as quietly as possible slide open the drawers to the white wall unit and felt around, glancing back occasionally to check. Adele was now descending the stairs, Sarah could make out each plod. She crouched and pulled open the cabinet doors and there, glistening on a plastic hook was a set of keys. She grabbed them from where they dangled. Adele's footsteps growing increasingly stronger. Sarah fumbled to get them in the lock and as Adele entered the room she could just see the door swinging back shut in the wind.

Sarah hurried up the suburban street. Any minute now Adele could come looking for her. She had grabbed a hoodie and some clean jeans out of a drawer in the room and now she pulled the hood up over her head. A bus was just arriving at the stop up ahead and Sarah ceased her moment to run and hop on. After paying for the same journey as the woman in front she swung down into a seat and retrieved the phone from her bag. Only now in relative safety had Sarah noticed how fast her heart was beating. She opened the Map app to identify where she was. Three stops later she was in the town flagging down a taxi and on her way home. She desperately hoped no one was there. As they approached the gate Sarah passed some crumpled notes to the driver and climbed out. The fob on her keys ignited the gate's mechanism and it retracted before her, she slipped through and jogged the long way down the drive. Sarah pressed for the garage door to open ignoring the main house and jumped into the Range Rover before reversing and screeching away.
She couldn't remember the way but luckily somewhere deep in her bag she retrieved the crumpled up piece of paper. It took fifty five minutes to get there and her phone had rung seven times. One of which was Macy. Sarah didn't

want to answer. She wanted to be alone, she wanted sometime, to make sense of things. She had drowned out the vibrating with the radio but now as she parked and jumped out there was no denying the shake of the phone in her hand. She clicked it off and knocked on the door. The music was the first thing she heard. Heavy metal, loud, really loud, as Ariel answered. She clicked on a remote and it stopped.

"Oh hi lady, come in. Sorry just listening to some soothing music to help me work"

"Sounds soothing" Sarah muttered as she strode past her and into the living room. "Have you got my phone?"

"Ok, calm down. Everything ok?" Ariel asked the woman standing in front of her, her hood still up she seemed clearly distressed.

"I just want the phone ok"

"Fine, fine. It's here, all done"

"Great" Sarah snatched it from the girl and clicked it into life. He hands trembled and her eyes began to fill with tears. She tried gritting her teeth against the wave of emotion but it was no use the tears fell down her cheeks.

"Hey lady, sit down please. Let me get you a drink, I'm good at coffee you know" Ariel joked as she guided Sarah onto the couch.

"I'm sorry" Sarah spluttered as Ariel returned with two steaming mugs "I'm just a mess, everybody is lying to me and I'm so confused. I don't even know who I am"

"That may just be the hormones" Ariel smiled weakly.

"What?" Sarah blinked.

She took the phone back from her and with a few clicks turned it round showing Sarah the image of a scan picture. Her mouth fell open.

"What the..."

"Congratulations" Ariel shrugged.

She spotted him in the waiting room, of course he was already there she thought to herself smiling. Gabrielle was beside him.

"Hi you two"

"Hey baby, I thought you were going to be late" Tom joked kissing her and rubbing her belly

"Oh God don't do that, my bladder is so full I may wet myself"

"What's new" Gabrielle laughed. Ava sat between them her hand firmly clasped in Tom's.

"I'm so excited" he beamed.

"I'm nervous" She said.

"Why?"

"You know just in case something is wrong, I'm not that young you know"

"Everything will be fine" Tom reassured.

"Ava Adams" the nurse called. The three of them rose.
"What? I'm coming too" laughed Gabrielle.
"Did we ever have any choice" Ava joked.
"Hello Ava, I'm Jenny, I'm your radiographer for today. Come on in, hop onto that bed for me. Great, now just lie back and expose your stomach for me"
There was a clear swelling to Ava's tummy and her breasts felt heavy, all good signs she thought.
"So is this your first baby?" Jenny asks smiling, while squeezing some gel on to Ava.
"Yes" she answered a flash of guilt bolted through her as Tom smiled down and clasped her hand.
"Sorry the gel is cold, right now let's have a look at your baby shall we?" Jenny smiled the dark cloud appearing on the fuzzy screen in front of her. As she pressed harder on Ava's stomach she fought the need to pee and in that empty black cloud appeared a small perfectly formed baby, its tiny heart fluttering and next to it an identical shape
"Wow baby! Look" Tom gasped, gripping her harder.
"Oh my god Ava!" Gabrielle squealed.
"Yes there you go, and as you may have gathered folks it seems you have two babies in there Ava" Jenny smiled.

It took a while but eventually John's heart rate had slowed
"Are you sure Macy?" he enquired and she nodded vigorously
"I memorised her number plate, it was her dad"
"Get my phone"
Macy looked around the room "I don't know where it is"
"What are you looking forward" Edward asked as he entered John's room.
"My phone" John answered.
"It is with Sarah, along with any other personal belongs, the previous hospital gave them to her" Edward added quickly.
"Sarah has my phone?" he demanded "What the fuck! Get me home now!"
"Dad?" Macy began to enquire before he put up his hand to silence her.
"This is why I am here John, everything is ready you will be transported home and offered round the clock care there. The porters are on their way to get you"
"Macy, you must find mum ok, get my phone and call your grandfather now"
Macy's hands trembled at the tone of her father's voice, she had never witnessed it from him before, although she had witnessed it earlier, at the hands of his father. She reluctantly dialled her grandfather's number and passed the phone to John.
"Leave us" he snapped at her.
"Fine I will go and find Eric" she snapped back confused.
His father answered on the third ring.

"Dad it's me. It was her. She did this to me"
The silence lasted only momentarily until the response came "Leave it to me" and the call was over. He turned to Edward still standing patiently in the room.
"Get me home" he growled "And let's hope this doesn't fall apart"
"There could be one more thing" Edward gulped "Adele made a mistake"
"What mistake?"
"She mentioned Gabrielle to Sarah"
Johns jaw dropped open, the heat of anger rose in him.
"What?" he spat.
"I'm sorry"
"I fucking told you not to leave her there, I knew Adele would break, I will have your balls for this Eddie"
Dr.Maxwell took one big step over to the bed so he towered over John and with clenched fists he spat back.
"Listen here, we are in this as deep as you to protect her, so don't threaten me. I'm stuck with Adele to keep your terrible secrets, unable to leave her and be happy because she blackmailed me by threatening to expose us. This has ruined my life too. Now I am going to get you home but if you continue to treat me like the enemy I will walk away from this John, do you understand?"
John couldn't speak. Never in his life had someone spoke to him with such venom and malice. He took a moment before smiling.
"You're the doctor"
He didn't notice the shake in Edwards hands as he left the room.

Sarah blinked at the image in front of her.
"Hey Sarah" Ariel sang waving her hand before her face "You were miles away"
"Sorry" Sarah mumbled. The memories were coming faster, they had more substance. She knew his face. Hell she knew his whole body and Gabrielle, she had remembered her as clearly as if the hospital appointment was merely this morning.
"So how far are you? This was a least two months ago" Ariel smiled brightly
"What?!" It took a moment to register "I'm not pregnant"
"Oh sorry, I just assumed it was you"
Sarah took the phone and clicked through her pictures, Tom. There he was all brimming with confidence and his familiar green eyed twinkle right in front of her, it wasn't a figment of her imagination, she wasn't confused, these memories were real. She swiped through numerous pictures of them some goofing around, some tender moments and then she stopped, the bright smiling face of Gabrielle, rubbing her slightly swollen stomach. Sarah gasped, the tears came again. There was a group shot of his family, the fleeting memory she once had of all the nieces and nephews and the brightly dressed mother. Purple and yellow. Sarah stifled a sob
"Here drink this" Ariel shoved the coffee under her nose "Take a minute"

"Thanks" Sarah took it and closed down the photos. The coffee was a warm and sweet welcome as the caffeine fix soared through her veins.

"What happened to Tom?" Ariel ventured.

"I, I don't know?"

"Well your text messages, as flirty and dirty as they are stop on the 31st August, you went to meet him at the 'new place' and then nothing" Ariel clicked open the messages app and the screen is full.

"Hey we could always just call him" Ariel offered.

Sarah looked at the young girl before her, phone him, that sounds like a dangerous idea but it piques her interest.

"I'll do it" Ariel grabbed the phone and hit the button. Before she can stop her it's done, Sarah holds her breath. The voice comes through almost instantaneously 'The number you have called cannot be recognised. Please check and try again'

"Shit" Ariel whispers.

"What about someone else?" Sarah stutters.

"Like who?"

"Gabrielle"

"Yeah her numbers in here. She text a lot, apparently you went AWOL."

"What do you mean?"

"She keeps asking where you are and to phone her. That it all makes sense" Ariel shrugs "I'll call her"

"No wait!" Sarah snatched the phone from Ariel. She needed to do this and alone "Thanks for your help but I need to be going" she tossed her the temporary phone

"Ok are you sure lady? I don't mind helping you?"

"No I can do it, thanks"

"Yes you can" Ariel answered smiling as Sarah fled from the house.

They wheeled him in carefully, the ride was uncomfortable and he was less than a good patient, and that was being kind. John Ryan was not only in pain, he was out of control, and that was a feeling none of the Ryan's relished. His parents were at the house to greet them and the hospital staff got him inside and comfortable on the lounge couch.

"Out! Everyone" demanded John Snr, and this time they all scarpered, even Rita.

"What the fuck is going on?"

"I don't know dad" John winced.

"I have him on the case. She will be found. You need a better bloody handle on this boy" his father boomed.

"Yes I know that, but I didn't factor her in"

"Well you bloody well should have. We can't have any of this unravelling, the business will suffer and well god knows what will happen to the deal let alone the future"

"Just find her, I will sort the rest"

"Mabel is sorting the launch"

"Mabel?"

"Well who the fuck else do you want in charge of it?"

"I fired Mabel father"

"Well I re hired her and since it's my company you will just have to jolly well get over it and learn to work with her"

"I can't! You know what she wants, she wants me out of here"

"There's another bastard mistake"

John Jnr gritted his teeth, he wasn't prepared to get into this with his father, the father who had fucked as many secretaries and interns as he had whiskeys which was a huge amount, and who to this day continued to be the poster boy for terrible husbands everywhere. The only ambition John had had growing up was to become as further away from the man his father was as possible, at this moment he wasn't convinced of his success

"Everything ok darling?" Rita peered through the doorway.

"Yes mother, fine"

"I wondered if I could help?" she stepped into the living room which now doubled as a hospital suite.

"What the hell could you do?" John snr sneered.

"I can't do this anymore" Rita began to sob "I can't risk my only son" she buried her face in her hands.

"Mother, please" John pleaded, he still hated to see her cry.

"Rita get it together"

"I can't I need to tell the truth, She did this and what's next? He's my son John" she shrieked. And then something happened, something that John Jnr hadn't witnessed for many years, something he hoped, but never quite believed had stopped. John Snr raised his hand high above his head brought it down on his wife. He struck her hard across her face with such force that it sent her hurtling to the ground, he marched over unrepentant and yanked her face up by her hair to strike her again. She screamed against it and John, confined to his seat protested loudly. John Snr turns on him, his mother's head still grasped in his hand

"Shut up or it's you next boy" and he resumed her beating.

"You will do as you are told" he shouted at her "Do you understand?"

He only relented, breathless, when she stopped struggling and pleaded she would do as he said.

"That is enough dad" John demanded. John Snr wiped his brow with his forearm and trudged out of the room. John Jnr turned away from his sobbing mother. Would she ever learn?

Chapter 18

She banged her fists on the steering wheel and screamed through her tears. The outside world was a blur, her only comfort was the sobs that expelled out, each one released a tiny fragment of frustration until eventually calming and grounding to a halt. Sarah sat and stared. She was still parked on Ariel's street and the phone lay motionless in her lap. She took it and got to Gabrielle's number, if anyone could give her answers it was Gabrielle, but something was holding her back, some undiagnosed reluctance. She knew what it was, it was him and them. John had been kind and loving, but mostly patient with her, he was the only life she knew at this moment. It was them, Macy and her humour, her graceful joy, she had been an ally and Eric, her double, had grown on her. Couldn't she just go home and accept her story, wouldn't this be easier. Her phone sprang to life. John.

"Hello"

"Hey honey it's me. I'm home and I wondered where you were and if you are ok?"

"Yeah I'm fine" she answered meekly.

"Are you sure? You sound a little down" he tried to muster a smile.

"John, you know you were in an accident last night right in front of us. I'm just still a little shaken that's all"

"Well I am home now, why don't you come home too, I think I may need you to help me, if you don't mind?" his voice sounded small, and there was a stirring of spousal concern within her.

"Sure honey, I'm on my way"

Rita sat with a bag of ice on her face dropping a few cubes into her gin and tonic. He hadn't hit her that fiercely for many years, although a light slap or passing kick was a regular occurrence. That's what wives endured her mother had once told her

"If you want nice things Rita, you have to pay for them. This is your price"

She glugged at her drink alone in the large pantry kitchen of their sprawling estate, the only light from above the Arga. John Snr had otherwise been a providing husband. Rita had received many gifts, a brooch here, a ring there, oh and the places he had taken her, the sumptuous hotels. This was normally from guilt, but the guilt had stopped years ago, and therefore so had the gifts. She had meant to leave him the night she lost her baby here in this very kitchen. Being in the oldest part of the house, the servant's quarters, the stairs down to it had always been steep and cut out of stone, uneven where, in the centuries before they wore thin from the commotion of feeding a wealthy family and all their guests. Easily slipped down, well that's what she told everyone afterwards, but she had remembered vividly the temper on his face as he flung her. As soon as she hit the concrete floor she felt the blood rush between her legs and she knew her baby girl was dead inside her. That was the end of the possibility of more children, which in itself had enraged another beating after they returned from the doctors. She had failed him in her one duty to, provide him with sons, plenty of healthy sons, and that's when John Ryan's guilt had ceased. In that moment on this very floor all those years ago Rita Ryan had took a steely determination and promised herself that her small, and only, sleeping son who was warm in his bed above her would never treat his wife the way John treated her. Her face stung as she moved the ice pack to another swollen part, she downed the gin and poured another with her free hand, before she took another sip she stared down the glass watching the bubbles fizz in the tonic below and realised she couldn't be sure if she had succeeded in that promise either.

The car silenced as she turned the key. Home, whatever that meant. The feeling couldn't be shook and she need time to read through her phone. "Fuck it" she spoke out loud as she hit dial on Gabrielle's number, she hesitated putting it to her ear holding it out a little so she could still hear but it was quiet, as if that protected her in some way. It rang. And it rang, and through the drumming of Sarah's heart she almost hit the end call button but the phone clicked and a familiar voice filled the car.

"What about this one?" she stroked down the edge of the grey wooden cot.
"Oh that's nice Gabs, it would go well in the new place" Ava said.
"What can I say, I have an eye for interior design, I should have a fucking empire with all my talent"
Ava slid her hand across the perfectly smooth side bar, a memory of the white cot she had built with him flashed through her mind.
"Maybe I should have a baby with John" she laughed.
"When are we going to get to meet this elusive John? You know Tom and I are starting to believe you are making him up" she teased.
"Shut up, I told you he travels, and he is going through a divorce so we have to take it slow, he exists though, believe me, I didn't imagine the pounding he gave me this morning, even I couldn't think up that!"
"Jesus Gabrielle, do we need every detail?" Ava smiled rolling her eyes, she was used to her crudeness but judging by the look the lady in front threw them, others definitely were not.
"I'm still sore! It's also a little aggressive you know"
"No I do not know, nor do I want to thank you!"
"It's almost as if his wife pisses him off so much and he just comes to mine and takes it out on my vagina"
The lady ahead tutted loudly.
"Maybe someone should take it out on her vagina" Gabrielle laughed

Sarah didn't leave a message. Instead she toyed with the memory again, she had a memory within a memory, of what though? That bit was frustratingly just out of reach. A white cot. That's all her brain was giving her to work on, great she thought.

He was dozing when she popped her head through the living room door, he looked peaceful on the large sofa. A nurse was monitoring his vitals on the machines that had been temporarily set up in their sprawling room.

"Does he need all these machines?" Sarah whispered as she approached.

"Oh yes. Just to keep on top of his heart rate and blood pressure. He had an internal bleed from the rib break, we need to make sure it doesn't happen again. Better safe than sorry"

"Jesus, should he not be in the hospital still?" Sarah folded her arms.

"Well yes, really he should, but we find patients of this, calibre shall we say, seem to get what they want" the nurse smiled warmly.

"Why don't you go get yourself a coffee or something I will sit with him?" Sarah offered.

"Ok great, I'm about done here anyway" and she slipped out of the room.

"Sarah?" he spoke.

"Hey honey, it's me I'm here. How are you feeling?"

"Like I've been hit by a bus!" he tried to laugh but the pain cut it short.

"Well not quite a bus, more like a sliver car" Sarah grinned at him and stroked his fair hair. He looked so vulnerable, yet still her heart swelled at the sight of him, she was taken aback by it.

"I wish I could kiss you" he grinned, it made her smile and blush, but she leant down a placed her lips ever so gently on his.

"I love you Sarah, you know that don't you?"

She nodded and she wasn't lying. She had known it the first night when she escaped out onto the drive way and he held her and promised to look after her. The mobile in her pocket vibrated and she stood bolt upright.

"Who's that honey?" he asked his head tuning slightly

"I don't know"

"Well, have a look" he smiled and nodded to her ringing pocket.

She swallowed as she reached in for it, she held it up to her face concentrating on not allowing him to see it wobble.

"Your mother" she lied.

"Ava is that you?" her voice was high but it sent flares of recognition throughout Sarah's body.

"Gabrielle?" she asked meekly.

"Oh my god it is you, I knew it, I knew it wouldn't work, they couldn't stop you. I knew you would call, where are you?" she spoke rapidly.

"I'm at home" she stuttered.

"Home? You're not at home, it's up for sale the flat, it's empty. If you're with him you need to leave now" she spoke with a frightening passion.

"What?"

"Ava you need to get out now you are in danger. Please trust me" she begged.

"What? I can't leave"

"Please you must, get out now I will tell you everything just meet me, there is a bar down the road"

"I can't, not now John's been in an accident"

There was silence on the other end of the phone.

"Gabrielle?"

"Yes I'm here. The accident it ….wait hey stop, who are you?" there was some commotion in the background.

"Gabrielle, hello?" Sarah whispered as loudly as she could.

"No stop, get off me" she screamed but the phone had clearly been dropped

"Ava" was all Sarah heard her shout in the background before some heavy breathing and the call ended.

They pulled up outside the cream limestone walls, it was dark but the evening air still held the heat of the day. Sarah grabbed a few crumpled euro notes and handed it to the taxi driver. Clambering out she fiddled for her keys before punching in the code allowing the gates to unfold, she slipped inside the courtyard, checking they closed behind her. The pool was bathed in artificial light, it threw just enough illumination to allow her to navigate the arches and guide her key into the lock to shut the world away. Sighing she dropped her bag and coat and she entered and headed straight to the kitchen to switch on some lights and open a bottle of wine from the well-stocked cellar. This was and had been her hideaway, her sanctuary, and she knew that tomorrow morning when John woke to the realisation that she was gone it wouldn't take long for him to figure out where she was. But until then she was alone, and she was glad of it.

Slumping into one of the brown leather sofas Sarah took a huge glug of her wine. Her heart ached, her head spun and the only way she knew how to deal with everything was to climb aboard a private jet and run away. The reality of what her life had become was too hard to face and she had to consider the children, what would Macy and Eric say? How would they even tell them? She internally chastised herself, worrying right now wasn't a solution, right now she would sit in peaceful silence and tomorrow she would pay Maria and Vinny a visit and they would help her figure all this out. She kicked off her shoes and edged down getting comfortable, she lay her head back and closed her eyes, but only momentarily for the knock at the door sent a chill down her spine. Sarah jumped up. No one knew she was here, she was careful to escape the house in England, and this house was fairly remote on the hills of Mellieha.

They knocked again. She placed the glass on the table and edged towards the door.
"Who is it?" She shouted her phone now clasped between her fingers.
"Open the door!"
Sarah yanked it open, her heart racing.
"John?"

The memory had took her breath away, Sarah gasped for air staring at the blank phone in her hand. She had remembered, the horror that Maria had told her in the toilets of their restaurant, Sarah had remembered. And the truth was terrifying.

His hand slipped round her mouth as she screamed and kicked. She could see the phone and just hear Ava shouting her, she felt was a slight scratch on the top of her arm and her eyelids became heavy, her body weighed more and more with each passing second. Gabrielle tried to fight against them both, the two masked men, but eventually all strength disappeared and she slipped into unconsciousness.
"Right, now she's more compliant, let's get her into the van quickly"
The other man simply nodded.
"Grab her feet"
They hoisted her up and checking the path was clear left her apartment and carried her swiftly down the fire escape stairwell and out into the back alley where the black van waited.
"Hurry up" the driver shouted tapping at the steering wheel, as they threw her limp body into the back he shouted "Oi be careful, boss said not damaged".
They slid shut the door with a clang, climbed in the front and the three men and one sleeping woman screeched away.

John was sleeping when he heard the vehicle pull up outside the living room window, he was yet to move off the couch. He waited as the door opened and the footsteps came closer. Everyone else was asleep he assumed, at least that's what his wife had told him when she stuck her head round the door earlier. She hadn't come in though, hadn't come close to him, he was almost suspicious that she didn't want to be near him, maybe she was afraid, yes that's what he had noticed in her eyes, that's what he knew instinctively was different, she had fear in her eyes. His father swung open the door "She called her"
"What?" John asked incredulously.
"How the fuck did she get her number? I thought this was dealt with."
"I, I don't know father. I took care of it, I did. This doesn't make any sense"
"Well clearly not, we just got to her in time. They heard them on the phone and moved in. We have her. But now the question is what do we do now?"

John shuffled painfully to sit up, he cursed her for this, not for causing him the pain but for paralysing him, and now it was beginning to unravel and he was confined to his own wincing.

"I need to see her"

"Absolutely fucking not"

"I'm our only hope"

"Really son? Crippled and in agony, I hope you're not otherwise we are screwed" "Where's Sarah?"

"Upstairs sleeping"

John Snr turned on his heels and marched out of the room ignoring the protests of his son. He climbed the stairs quietly, creeped down the landing past Macy's room and pulled down on the handle to the master bedroom. He opened it gently, his eyes adjusting to the lack of light the bed came into focus. Empty. He burst into the room, scanning for any sign of her, he burst into every bedroom only to find those empty too. With clenched fists he marched back downstairs and out into the garage where John's Range Rover was missing.

Chapter 19

"You haven't spoken to me all day, please I'm sorry, I didn't really tell her anything"

He pulled back the duvet and slipped between the sheets. She ran a hand up his exposed arm but he flinched away from her.

"Please Edward" Adele begged.

"Do you know what you have possible done Adele? Do you understand how this affects us? What it will do to our family?"

"I'm sorry" she began to cry and buried her head in her hands "I'm so sorry, I never wanted to let you down".

He sighed, as angry as he was he didn't like to see her cry, he had caused enough of that over the years and it still ignited the guilt within him. He sat up and put his arm around her.

"Shhhhh its ok" he soothed "We will just have to fix it, to deal with it"

"How?" She looked up at him her tears subsiding.

"Weave ourselves further into this web of deceit" and he forced a smile. Adele wiped her eyes, seemingly placated by his answer, the strap of her silk nightdress slipped down her arm and he retrieved it for her.

"Thanks" she smiled.

"I'm sorry I missed the boys recital, again" he offered "The Ryan's are taking over my life"

"It's ok" she sniffed "today I understand"

He pushed back her dark hair to reveal her face, gently tilting her head up by her chin. She eventually looked at him and smiled meekly. Cautiously he took the same strap he had just replaced and pushed it down over her shoulder. It seemed funny to him that he didn't think anything of fucking Clara but of his wife he was less confident. She let it slide all the way down feeling the sensation of the silk slipping over her nipple. Spurred on by her willingness he took the other strap and pushed that away until she sat before him fully exposed the nightdress crumpled in the lap of her crossed legs. He hardened swiftly under the sheets, the desire for her surging through his groin. She remained motionless. Carefully he stroked her breast watching intently for her reaction, she welcomed him, after all it wasn't very often he took her. Slowly climbing on top of her he leaned his face down to kiss her gently and as she opened her thighs willingly Edward slid inside his wife.

She was hurtling down the road, tears following freely down her cheeks, desperate sobs escaping through her gritted teeth. The windscreen wipers squeezed frantically against the downpour. She may not remember much but what she did was slowly beginning to piece things together, and it terrified her. His keys had been the closest to grab and she had no idea how to slow down the wipers, searching through the levers on the steering wheel she almost ploughed into the oncoming truck, swerving to miss it marginally. Her heart pounded as she pulled over and turned off the engine. Her phone vibrated. John. The thought of talking to him sickened her.

"What are you doing here?" She stuttered closing the door behind him
"Me? What are you doing here more importantly? Slipping away in the middle of the night?"
"How did you know?" She asked wide eyed
"You didn't think you could charter a plane without them telling me? I was on one straight behind you, I could almost see you in the sky ahead" he smirked menacingly. She followed him into the living room as he picked up her discarded glass and downed her wine. "Looks like we need a top up" he sauntered off into the kitchen.
"Please John, I just wanted to have a break, I need a break" she muttered. He pulled the cork out of the bottle with a pop and it made her jump. She shook out her hands. He stared at her as he poured, the liquid glugging into the glass, he downed that too.
"Want one?" He put the glass up too her, she shook her head.
"Well you were drinking before, don't let me kill the party"
She shook her head again, her eyes firmly on the floor
"So how is Tom?" He asked.
He heart stopped. It knocked the wind from her.
"Oh you think I don't know! Oh my dear, I know everything" he smirked walking round to her, she instinctively took a step back which only broadened his smile. He managed to catch her chin in his hand and he squeezed it hard. Towering over her he scrutinised her face turning it one way and then the next.
"Please, you're hurting me" she tried to pry away his fingers but his force becoming all the more crushing.
"Well you are hurting me. You think I'm just going to let you break up this family because of a little fling?"
"I'm not the only one in this marriage having a little fling, in fact I'm am the only one having just one!"
Her eyes stung but she gritted her teeth not wanting to show weakness, by the sound of his small chuckle he had already sensed it, fear in his prey. He pressed his mouth down hard on hers and prised her clamped lips open with his tongue. She pushed at him with both her arms managing to shove him back marginally earning her a momentary reprise. Then she felt the full force of his hand across her jaw, she stumbled backwards. The sting came immediately.
"Looks to me like someone is up for some fun" he joked.
"No stop please" she backed away from him tripping back over the table, his eyes twinkled as she nearly fell, managing just to stay on her feet. He placed down the glass he was holding and grabbed her arm yanking her violently

towards him, he snatched her hair in his hands tipping her head back and continued to kiss her. She squirmed against him trying to free herself, shouting for him to stop, and then he hit her again, hard in the face. The shock silenced her, her hand flying up to the blood now pouring from her nose, and he threw her face down onto the couch

"This will go much better for you if you stop struggling Sarah" he sang as he punched her again, she screamed out but he kept hitting her over and over again as she turned her exposed ribs away from him and assumed the foetal position. He stopped to undo the belt of his trousers slipping it off in one swift movement he brought it down on her, she yelled out.

"John stop"

"Is he worth it Sarah?" He demanded as he whipped her again.

"No please stop" she sobbed. He bent down and pushed her face into the leather of the sofa, she could hardly breathe, it was all a blur and her body screamed in pain, she felt him kick apart her legs, terror rose inside her. She tried desperately to wriggle free but he landed the hardest hit of all in her side knocking the fight from her. He ripped down her trousers, she felt the air on her exposed buttocks, still he pushed her head face down into to seat. He slapped her arse hard, once, twice, three times as her muffled cries stiffened his cock harder than he had experienced for years. She could hardly breathe through the pain and the force in which she was being held down. She just wanted it to be over, instantly as she felt him slam inside her she shut her eyes tight.

She only just opened the door in time to vomit on the pavement. The nausea was dizzying. She heaved again, and again, producing lime green liquid to splatter a top the contents of her stomach already pasted on the floor. Sarah needed a plan. Scrambling through the glove box to find a tissue to wipe away the remnants of her disgust her fingers patted and curled around something cold and hard. The muscles in her body tensed with recognition and she froze momentarily before sliding it out and resting her gaze on the black screen. He has another phone. She gulped, mostly to stop the gag reflex threatening to send her into painful convulsions again, and clicked the phone into life. This one had no passcode, strange she thought, but then maybe this one was never supposed to be found. Trembling Sarah opened the three unread emails.

Subject: Payment From British Gas
Thank you for your recent payment received. We have issued instructions for someone to monitor your gas usage.
Please note we will inform you of any changes
Mr R. Ares

Subject: Urgent Visit
It seems there have been some issues with your boiler and we would like to call to discuss. Please advise a suitable time.
Mr R. Ares

Subject: British Gas Head Office Visit
Thank you for your recent correspondence, we have followed instructions and now await your immediate visit to Head Office to discuss the outcome of our findings
Mr R. Ares

Sarah gawped at the screen. She blinked away tears of betrayal, something told her this was nothing to do with British Gas, but what is was she had no clue. The phone in her hand sprung into life, starling her. No caller ID. She picked up quickly and held it too her ear without speaking.
"John?" the woman's voice started "John is that you?"
Sarah recognised the voice before she clicked off and the line went dead, and she knew just the person to help.

The vast room seemed drowned in a yellowish light originating from the small black box atop a lone desk. It felt cold. Her head bobbed to one side as her eyes caught the blackness of large windows across a huge brick wall, the rust of the steel columns with their incredible rivets, the dust on the concrete floor. One of the men laughed at the black box. Her mind was tired and muggy as she slowly began to regain consciousness, the two men coming steadily into focus. Gabrielle's heart began to pound in her chest. The urge to jump up and run away soared through her but for some reason she wrestled with it, wanting to remain still, remain invisible.
They were watching Happy Days, unmasked but facing away from her. One man rested his feet on the desk whist the other leant forward in his chair pouring boiling water into a noodle snack, he sat back and slurped some into his mouth.
"Fuck"
The other turned to him "It will still be hot you daft bastard"
"No shit". They returned to their amusement as Gabrielle quietly lifted her head. A warehouse, she was in a warehouse. Sat on a hard chair her arms bound behind her, as she pulled hard against the tape on her wrists it gave just a little, but stuck fast. The terror was building inside her. Who were these men and why did they have her. She focused on controlling her breathing, convinced that the banging of her pulse would be heard even over the Fonz and Chachi. Scanning the room to try to establish any clue of where and why she was here a phone rang and she jumped, hearing the squeak of her chair against the floor the two men shot around only to find their charge still unconscious

"Hello? Yeah we are still here. She's out. What you want us to do when she wakes? Ok. You're coming here? We will up her dose till then"

Gabrielle squeezed her eyes tight.

"Grab another syringe"

"Are you sure it will be alright to give her more? You know how things go with this lot, look at the mess we had to clean up last time"

"Just grab the fucking needle. Doc said as long as we didn't give her more than one at once it would be fine"

"But what about the time?"

"Shut the fuck up and pass it me"

She was paralyzed with fear. They couldn't know she was awake but they were going to administer more drugs. Gabrielle did the only thing she could. Stay perfectly still and let sleep take her from this place.

The car had been almost abandoned in the deserted street. Sarah banged on the door until, eventually it was yanked open and a dishevelled looking Ariel squinted against the nightly hour.

"What the fuck lady?"

Sarah pushed in past her and slammed the door.

"I need your help"

Ariel followed her down the hallway and into the living room and listened as Sarah paced up and down.

"I have to find somebody and I have to find them now, this is a mess, it's a fucking mess. Shit!" she pulled back her hair "I have this" Sarah held the phone out to Ariel, still rubbing her eyes against the sleep desperate to claim her "There's some emails, can you find where they are from? I mean exact place, a location?"

Ariel took the phone and opened it. She silently headed into the kitchen and flicked on the kettle. Throwing down the phone she fished two mugs out from the dirty sink and began to wash them.

"Hey. Can you do this?" Sarah snapped.

Ariel turned to her, her shoulders fell "Jesus, of course I can fucking do it, don't you know that by now. Its gonna take a while so sit down, I'll make us a coffee"

"Right. Ok. Great" Sarah sat, drumming her fingers on her lap "So how long is a while?"

"Depends how well they hid themselves, could be an hour could be longer. I will know soon enough. What's going on anyway? Actually scrap that. I don't want to know"

Chapter 20

Edward was used to being summoned at all hours by his high level patients, after all they paid him enough to afford his large five bedroom Victorian villa and the apartment overlooking the water he kept for Clara. This felt different, he knew it instantly, mostly by the fact it was John Snr that called. Macy had rushed downstairs at the sound of the car, she recognised it immediately as she dashed to the window, sleep hadn't come even now, settled in her own bed something was niggling at her. The door opened and Edward had stepped only one foot on the hall tiles and Macy was in front of him, her face ashen.

"What's wrong? Why are you here?" she asked the panic bring her voice up at the end.

"Hi Macy, nothing to worry about, I'm just checking your Dad's medication, he's not on the right dose I think"

"Really is that all? Are you sure?" she searched his eyes.

"Are you ok Macy?" he put his hand on her shoulder, she shifted her weight

"It's late, why are you still up?"

"I can't sleep"

"Really? For how long?" He stooped down to look into her eyes.

"I'm fine Edward honestly, I'm just, restless"

"You should come into the practice tomorrow anyway, get checked over"

"No" she dismissed him "I'm ok. Just a crappy few days"

"Well try to rest ok, I'm going to check on your father"

As Edward finished his statement the large oak door at the end of the vast hallway opened and John Snr appeared. Macy's brow furrowed, Johns face hardened at the sight of his granddaughter.

"What are you doing up? Get back to your room" he barked at her. Macy turned to look at Edward.

"Please let me know how Dad is when you are finished? I'll be upstairs"

He nodded in response having born witness to a passing between the relatives before him, but of what he was unsure.

"Ready?" John Snr ushered as Edward cleared his throat once Macy was safely out of ear shot.

"Yes" he muttered heading through the open door and into the lounge where John Jnr sat his eyes wide

"We think she is remembering" John Snr whispered as he silently closed the door.

"What?" Edward looked between the two men, John Jnr nodded slightly.

"How do you know?" Edward asked.

"She called Gabrielle" John Snr spoke as he sat on the large grey couch, he huffed moving some of the cushion's, affording him the ability to lean back. His hands fell loosely over his crossed legs as he challenged Edward with his stare. Edward slumped into the chair opposite him, his head in his hands.

"How much? How much do you think she remembers?"

"It doesn't matter much does it, you told us she wouldn't remember anything" John Snrs face tilted as he spoke again calmly.

"John?" Edward turned to face her husband, clearly in discomfort between them

"I don't know. She hasn't really spoke to me" he mumbled.

"Well that's great son, way to keep your wife under control"

"She is not a fucking possession, what do you want me to do?" he spat back at his father.

"That's not important, what's important here is what the hell we are going to do now?" John Snr aimed his words at the doctor.

"I don't know. I warned you this was a risk. It's not a proven drug, it's difficult to administer, the trauma may not have helped. I couldn't guarantee success with this, I told you that"

"Well you need to fix it"

"How?"

"I don't know, I'm not the medical professional, and if you don't fix it, neither will you be" John Snr's eyes narrowed and Edward understood all too well the truth in that threat.

"Can you talk to her John? Maybe it's best to tell the truth, kind of, embellish but give her the key points. Where is she?" Edward asked her husband.

"We don't know" John Snr snapped staring at his son.

"I have tried to call her, she won't answer. I have no idea who she could be with, or where"

"Maybe it's time to call Adele" Edward offered "She told her they were friends"

"What?" John leant forward in his chair "What else did your wife tell her?"

"Nothing!" Edward's hands flew up defensively "Nothing at all, just they used to be friends before the accident. Maybe she can phone Sarah and maybe if Sarah see's it's her she will answer"

"Can't, I wiped all the numbers in her phone" John Jnr chimed in.

"Well fuck. Excellent work again son"

"Listen dad, can you drop the attitude this isn't my fault"

"Well maybe if you hadn't fucked up with Mabel..."

"Mabel?" John interrupted.

"Yes Mabel, think I don't know about the affair?"

"I'm sorry?" John leaned forward the drugs clearly helping his mobility.

"You had an affair with Mabel"

John almost choked "What? My affair with Mabel?"

"I know everything" His father growled.

The rain was beating at the window as Ava nursed her mug of tea. The café was full but she couldn't hear a thing. She wasn't aware of the clang of cutlery, the spit of steam, the mumbling chatter, the scrape of chairs and mindless lives being lived out behind her. She was however acutely aware of the way her trousers pulled around her slightly swollen stomach and how her breasts ached in her bra. She swallowed hard, unsure if she could find the words and with each second that ticked on the large antique clock hanging on the wall her heart drummed faster, if it was a race her heart was winning. Her blank stare continued to drift up the busy street outside, not falling on to anything in particular, the raindrops blurring the faces of those passing, the beeping of horns muffled by Ava's overwhelming thoughts. He was going to be here soon. Reaching down to wrap her hands around her luke warm, half-drunk cup, a flash of familiarity out of the corner of her eye caused her heart to lurch. Focusing on the woman climbing out of a cab across the street, Ava had to dodge the raindrops cascading down the window for a clear view, she had her hood up, Ava squinted. A man climbed out after her, the woman turned to him a broad smile across her face the red curls escaping, billowing in the wind. She laughed and kissed the man before he disappeared back into the car and she ran inside the department store opposite. That must be him, the elusive John England, as the car drove away Ava tried to catch a glimpse, her brow furrowed.

"Hey" Tom rested his hand on her shoulder and she jumped.

"Jesus, you scared me" her hand flew to her stomach.

"Oh sorry baby" he chuckled siting opposite "I just saw Gabrielle across the street, is she joining us?" he gestured for the waitress.

"No. I didn't know she was going to be here"

"Small place London sometimes. Can I have a coffee please, black thanks" he ordered "So how are you feeling?" he lifted her hand to kiss it and her tummy dropped. Ava offered him a meek smile.

"I'm ok. We're ok" she rubbed her belly.

"That's good, I missed you this morning"

She laughed, taking a long hard look at this beautiful man before her, whose effervescent green eyes light up when he saw her. She was about to blow their perfect life to shreds and he had no clue.

"Me too" She muttered "Tom, I have something to tell you and it's really difficult, but I want you to hear me out, ok? Listen till the end?"

His stunning smile slipped only marginally, he tilted his head to one side "Ava, you are scaring me"

"Please promise you will listen till the end?" she sat up as straight as she could, as hard as this was going to be, being away from them was only supposed to be temporary, it had been five months already and she needed them like this earth needed the rain running down the pane beside her.

"Ok baby I promise" he sat back in his purple velvet chair, he crossed one thick leg over the other. He was in a tracksuit having just been with a client this morning and Ava thought how sexy she found him. She coughed pushing the thought of what she could potentially loose to the back of her mind, nothing was more important to her than them. She caressed her belly again. She made the decision to blurt it out, took a deep breath and said
"I'm married. I have two children already and I left because I was raped"

Ariel worked, flitting from one device to another as Sarah tried to stop the bounce in her leg. That awful day was coming back to her. The way she loved Tom was seeping in, and she needed him. Where was he? The phone rang.
"Expecting someone?" Ariel looked up at Sarah for the first time in over an hour
"No. Who is it?"
"Hang on" and with a couple of clicks all Adele's details came up on Ariel's screen "Adele Maxwell, know her?"
"Shit Ariel this is some MI5 stuff you have right here? You can find all this out in a few seconds?" Sarah gawped at the screen.
"It amazing how much information is held about people online, if you know how to find it" she said her gaze not moving from Sarah.
"He must know I'm not there. I bet he called and asked her to phone me thinking I will answer now I know we used to be friends"
Ariel cancelled off the call "Come on we are busy, I've nearly got them, they know what they are doing I'll give em that, not some cowboy outfit here. Shit"
"What?"
"Nothing, don't worry just another minor detour, each time I get close it re-routes me"
"Are you sure you can…"
Ariel shot Sarah down with a look and returned to her incessant clicking and tapping on the computer.
"Got cha! Ha fuck you motherfuckers! Victory is mine! Here ya go, two devices, one mobile which I'm tracing and the other at this address"
Sarah shot out of her seat and stuck her face into the bright glare coming from the screen. Albion Wharf. That sounded familiar. She racked her brain.
"Can you print me that address?"
"Sure" the printer whirred into life "Just got a hit on the mobile device, it's there too, probably sitting right next to each other"
"Thanks" Sarah snatched the paper out of her hand.
"Wait" Ariel shouted "Let me throw some clothes on"
"What?" Sarah turned, halfway out of the room.
"You think I'm sitting this one out? Whoever they are they are good, and you are going to need me"

There was a small tap at the door, Macy turned over.

"Come in"

Eric's face appeared in the gap.

"Hey bro!" Macy sat up and gestured for Eric to lie in the bed with her.

"I can't sleep" he said climbing in beside her.

"Me either" She slid down in the bed until they were facing each other.

"Do you know where mum is?"

"She's asleep I think"

"She isn't Mace, I went in to find her"

"What?"

"She's not in her room and I snook downstairs to try to find her. That's when I overheard voices in the living room, dad, grandad, Edward"

"Yeah Edward came to check on dads meds"

"No. They were talking about drugs and how mum was remembering and she shouldn't be"

"What?" Macy gasped "What are you talking about?"

"I don't know, something weird is going on. They don't want her to remember"

"Would you? All the arguments? The tension"

"No Macy. It's more than that, I think they made her forget"

"What?"

"And there's something else. Dad was having an affair"

There was another small rapping at the door. They both froze as it creaked open.

"Hi, oh Eric good, I'm glad you are both here. Mind if I come in?" Edward asks smiling.

"No, come in please, how's Dad?" Macy sat up again her head reeling from Eric's words. Edward sat on the edge of the bed.

"Dad is struggling a little here, we have agreed to take him back to the hospital"

"That's not true..." Eric tried to cut in but Macy silenced him with a swift stare.

"Eric?" Edward asked shifting closer.

"Ignore him, he's sleepy and confused" Macy offered.

"It's absolutely nothing to worry about" Edward tried to comfort "Will you be ok here? Or do you want me to take you to Adele?"

"No its fine. We will be ok, just sort Dad out and will you please call me in the morning?" Macy answered.

"Of course. Sleep well you two. You call me if you need anything you know Adele is only a short drive away"

"Its fine thanks"

He nodded, kissed them both and with one last look closed the door behind himself.

"They're not taking dad to hospital Mace" Eric whispered frantically "They are going to get Gabrielle"

"Gabrielle?" Macy enquired.

"She's the woman I think, with the red hair. The one who ran over dad"

"You saw that? You knew it was her?"

"Yes" he averted his eyes "I knew, and what's more Mace is that grandad knows dad was having an affair and thinks it was with Mabel. But I don't. I think it was with her. With Gabrielle"

"What makes you think that?"

"I saw them" Eric looked back up into the wide eyes of his sister.

"Wait!" Sarah halted, the realisation almost taking her legs from beneath her, as they both headed out the door minutes later "You know all that information you found on Adele"

"Yes?" Ariel whispered her key in the lock, not wanting to wake her housemates.

"Could you find it on Tom?"

"Well yes, now we have his number"

"Even though it's no longer in use?" Sarah enquired.

"Really Sarah, do we have to keep going over this! Of course I can"

"Well then could you?"

Ariel looked to the door and back to the clearly distressed woman in front of her.

"Now?" She asked.

Sarah took a moment to weigh up the options, Gabrielle could be in danger, but here tantalisingly close, so could Tom.

"Yes now" there was no competition.

"Alright then" Ariel removed the key from the lock leading the swiftly back to the living room.

"But hurry" Sarah added.

"Jeez lady, you don't want much do you?"

Ariel plugged Sarah's phone in and hit the keys. Her face once again illuminated in illegal light. She typed and bashed and typed. Her face fell, confusion radiating across it.

"Ariel?" Sarah started.

"Strange hang on"

Ariel continued hitting the keys, her fingers moving with rapid urgency, the clicking culminating in a technological crescendo, she sat back in the seat and turned to Sarah.

"What? What is it?" Sarah panicked.

"I don't know how to tell you this" Ariel's eyes softened.

"Tell me what? Just say it"

"He's deceased"

Sarah's legs collapsed beneath her.

The yellowish light called her again from deep within her induced slumber, the re run of Happy Days failed to allude to any passage of time. The two men were laughing haughtily as she fought desperately for consciousness. Her mouth was dry and her body ached for fluid, this was the only indication that she had been there a while, even though the darkness of night still streamed in through those large windows. Nausea hit her, saliva began to congregate in her mouth, her stomach churned. Again she fought desperately, but she couldn't win this battle, her body expelled the contents of her stomach across the concrete floor.

"Jesus fucking Christ" one of the men said startled by the noise of her retching.

"Fuck. Get the mop will ya, we gotta move her. How much was in that needle?"

"What the doctor put in there Roge"

"Well it maybe more than she can handle"

Gabrielle heaved again as more liquid spewed out of her. Then she sat back, empty, she was done.

"Finished now love?" the tallest man asked "Get her arms"

They grabbed her limp body under each arm pit and hoisted her onto a scabby old couch. Gabrielle welcomed the lie down even with her hands and feet still bound.

"Please some water?" she croakily begged. The smaller guy complied.

"Clean that mess up" Roge demanded as Gabrielle took a big slurp of water, the cool freshness relieving.

"Boss, cars incoming" the headlights flashed across a large screen next to where Happy Days still played. The tall guy marched over as survey the scene.

"It's them" he answered "Nothing to worry about, but hurry clean her up, they won't be happy if she's in this state. Unharmed remember"

He wiped her face quite gently with a cloth and even though he tried to sit her up her protesting groans required him to leave her be.

Roger strode over to the lift, pressing the button that sent it down. He click a fuzzy radio into life

"Clients imminent, let them pass"

A clear voice burst through the fizz "Roger that boss"

She turned the handle and slowly entered their flat unsure of the greeting awaiting her, of even that there was one until she heard his humming along to Stevie Wonder. She threw her keys down on the table in the small hallway and his head popped out from the kitchen doorway.

"Hi" she offered. He didn't respond, he just disappeared and continued to hum. Ava sighed. He was here at least. That was more than she had hoped for. She paused at the doorway, he was stirring something delicious in a pot on the stove. He still wore the tracksuit from earlier only he has discarded the jacket, and stood in a white T-shirt bearing the embroidery of his website on the back and the fluffy pink slippers Ava had bought as a joke a while back.

"Smells gorgeous" she mumbled. He tensed at her words "Tom please..."
"Just go and sit down Ava" he stated the humming now over as he clicked off the iPod.
"Please talk to me?"
He turned to her "Go and sit down" he demanded, her shoulders dropped, as did her gaze and she turned to head into the living room. The table was set, candles flickering, dancing light around the room. The two crystal wine glasses next to a bottle of fizzy water helped choreograph the performance. She gasped. This was the last thing she expected. Tom appeared behind her with two bowls, he raised his chin in the direction of the table.
"Go. Sit" he said. She dropped her bag and slipped off her mac as she complied. He placed the bowls down and dropped into the seat opposite.
"Now I have something to tell you, and I want you to promise to listen to the end now ok?"
She nodded, the candlelight reflected in his serious green eyes.
"What you told me today was a shock, and I am sorry I walked out..."
"It's ok" she interrupted.
His face darkened "Till the end you promised!" he groaned.
"Sorry, I'm sorry. I won't say another word"
Silence hung between them for a moment as they searched each other's faces, pain winced in his. "What you told me today" he began again "was a shock and I have been processing it all afternoon. I thought this baby was our first, the first journey into parenthood together"
Ava opened her mouth to say something but his look forced her down.
"I can't say I'm not a little disappointed that is isn't, and you lied to me. A huge big whopping lie. And I don't know the details, but I get it"
Ava looked up "You do?"
"Yes" he sighed "And I love you and our baby"
"I love you too" she spluttered, a tear running down her cheek.
"So we are going to figure this out, because this" he lifted her left hand and the diamond adorning her third finger sparkled "I meant it when I gave you this, I meant forever. I forgive you, you went through a horrendous thing and I want to build you back up and take care of you"
"You already have" she sobbed.
"No all of you, Macy and Eric and our little ones. Whatever it takes I'm here for you"
Ava leapt out of her seat and dashed into Toms welcoming embrace. He held her tightly as she kissed him through her tears. Her heart had lifted and underneath her blouse she felt a familiar thud.
"Quick, here" she took Toms hand, sitting on his knee she lifted her shirt and placed it on her bare rounded stomach. The thud came again.
"Wow" Tom laughed "That was a strong one"

"Yes it was" Ava smiled at him as she kissed him again. With the absence of further movement his hand moved up from her stomach to her breast, caressing the round fullness of it. Ava moaned in response. His fingers expertly unbuttoned her top, her mouth still frantically bearing down on his, she wriggled free of her shirt as it floated to the floor. He reached around to release her bra as both breast bounced free. He drank in the sight her large dark nipples, the veins running clear across the surface of her heavy boobs.

He lifted her easily, even with the additional weight of her stomach and took her still half naked into their bedroom. He placed her down gently laying a kiss on her exposed stomach as he softly pulled down her pants, expertly taking her knickers with him. He yanked the t-shirt over his head, and pushed down his bottoms stepping out of them and taking a moment to stand proudly over the beautiful pregnant woman lay in front of him.

"You are so gorgeous" he hummed, his huge erection confirming his desire.

"So are you" Ava said.

The phone rang and Tom growled.

"Ignore it" Ava panted.

"This is getting weird Ava, I'm telling you, someone is watching us"

"It's nothing" she moaned.

"Could it be him?" Tom's mouth turned down, Ava froze. This was the first time he knew. She just shrugged. He strode over to the phone and picked up the handset without saying anything.

"Do not put your dick in my wife. You want Macy and Eric. You want your own child. Bring Sarah. Ryan Warehouse, Albion Wharf. Eleven tonight" the line went dead.

Tom turned to Ava.

"What? Who was it?" she held her breath.

"I guess it was him, wanting someone called Sarah. Ava, who is Sarah?"

She looked away *"Me"*

John winced as he climbed out of the car. He held onto the arm still strapped in a sling, Edward looked questioningly at him.

"I'm fine" John brushed him off.

"Are you sure you don't want more pain relief?"

"No I'm good" he assured closing the door with his good arm. The three men marched through the darkness to the entrance in silence, only the crunch of gravel beneath their feet betrayed any evidence of them being there. They knocked and the door opened instantly.

"Mr Ryan"

The old man pushed through leading the way. The lift was waiting and the three, still silent climbed inside. The welcome party, his thighs holding a M1911 on each leg, pulled closed the grate, hit the button and they began their assent.

"Just to be clear I don't want any harm to come to Gabrielle, we are already in enough shit father" John spat.

"Fine" his father conceded.

"You let me speak to her"

"Fine" he answered again.

"I know what to do"

"Really?" John Snr turned to him an eyebrow raised.

"If I didn't have an arm in a sling I would punch you right now" John Jnr spat and Edward jumped between the men before this could escalate any further. Gladly the lift came to an abrupt halt and a man yanked open the grates.

"Roger" John Jnr acknowledged as he stepped first out of the lift "Where is she?"

Roger nodded over to the couch.

"Jesus it smells like sick in here" John said.

"Yea she hasn't been good boss" Roger answered.

John looked to Edward, he nodded and rushed over to Gabrielle as she lay mumbling on the couch. He checked her pulse, shone a light in her eyes and opened the case he was carrying, produced a syringe and administered the liquid.

"What is that?" John Snr barked "Actually I don't want to know"

"It's adrenaline, she is ok, she will be fully awake soon" Edward answered.

John ordered a chair to be placed in front of Gabrielle, and as she came round, her vision focused, she whispered "John?"

"Hey baby" he answered.

"Don't fucking hey baby me you lying piece of shit"

"Gabs I suggest you calm down"

"Calm fucking down, you took her and what the fuck is going on here hey? I'm dragged out of my apartment and drugged, do you know how many fucking laws you are breaking!"

"Well that's rich coming from you" John leant back and smirked.

"What do you mean?"

"Look at me Gabrielle, I know you did this, I know it was you"

She froze "Prove it" she spat.

"Well, if you play ball, you are going to wake warm and safe in your bed and you won't be able to prove this either, so I guess we are evens"

"And If I don't play ball?" she snapped.

John sighed. His father listening intently over his shoulder.

"Well that would be a bad move"

"There are things going on here you don't understand" John Snr interjected.

"Like what? And can you take this fucking things off me?" she demanded nodding towards her still bound hands and wrestling on the couch. John Jnr paused and then nodded as her two captor's rallied round to release her.

"No funny business Gabs" John snapped as she rubbed at her wrists "Now are you prepared to listen?"

She sat back and folded her arms "This should be good"

"The woman you know is not Ava. Her name is Sarah and she is my wife"

"I guessed that, you cheating prick. Is that another reason she left you? And then you used me to follow her?"

"Look you have every right to be angry, I did use you to find her and watch her, but she is my wife, the mother of my children and I needed to bring her home"

"Home? She had a home, and a life, wait... Those children are Ava's?" Gabrielle was startled.

"Yes and she left them"

"Well we all know why she left them, why she left you, don't we John?" Gabrielle spat.

"Why is that Gabrielle?"

"Enough of this bullshit son, give her the terms and let's get out of here" John Snr interrupted "I hate doing this dirty work myself"

"Wait I want to hear this. Why Gabrielle, why do you think she left me?"

"Because you raped her" she hissed.

Outside they told the taxi to turn off his lights and follow slowly. They had lost the car up ahead but guessed it had turned off around here.

"Actually we will get out now" Macy announced handing the driver a bunch of notes.

"Thanks" she answered dragging a confused Eric with her and closing the car door quietly. The taxi man nodded and turned to speed away not keen on the idea of being dragged into whatever mess these kids where creating.

"Why here Mace?" he asked looking down at the industrial estate surrounded by blackness. There was no hint that anyone was here.

"Because I know where they are"

"You do? Where?"

"This was Grandads old head office" She pointed to the large building at the back "They changed it to a warehouse when Dad took over the business, I used to play here as a child"

"You did?"

"Yes, and that means I know just how to sneak in" she grinned through the moonlight "Come on bro follow me" she headed across the field and down the hill their footsteps silenced by the grass.

"This is not a good idea Tom" Ava wringed her hands as they approached the industrial estate bathed in darkness.

"Do you want them back Ava? Sarah? Whatever your name is" he faced forward eyes straight out over the steering wheel.

"How did he sound, on the phone?"

"I told you, pissed off I was about to fuck his wife"

"I'm not his wife anymore"

"Oh really? Really baby, can you show me your divorce papers?"

She turned to face out the window, hiding her tears.

"I mean did he sound young or old?"

"What? I don't know, he sounded pissed. And I would be too. We need to sort this out, so we can move on. What were you going to do, stand up in a church and sign your name as Ava Adams? And just lie to me"

"Tom please" she begged.

"No not Tom please, you need to tell me"

"I. I don't know. But you know why, please, please don't be mad at me" she held her stomach and he saw the gesture. He sighed.

"I just want the truth. I want to tell him it's over and whatever spying shit he has on us needs to stop before I go to the police"

"No!" Ava stresses *"No police"*

"Why the fuck not, why not report it"

"Because I can't ok, it would ruin everything"

"Everything is pretty ruined from where I am standing"

"Not for us, for them"

"Who?"

"Macy and Eric" the names on her lips made her heart ache. The babies wriggled inside her as if they recognised their siblings.

"Does Gabrielle know?" Tom challenged the notion just dawning on him *"Did she come with you from that life, does she know all about Sarah and her secret family?"*

"No! She only knows I was married and why I left"

"What? You told her and not me?"

"No! She found my ring once, right at the beginning of our friendship of me being Ava, she found it in a drawer when she came round. So I just told her parts. She doesn't know my name is Sarah"

Tom's muscles in his jaw clenched.

"I'm sorry, please try to understand" Ava pleaded running her hand up his outstretched arm. His shoulders relaxed at her touch.

"I am" he said through gritted teeth *"I really am"*

"We will be ok wont we?" Ava asked as they pulled up at the familiar building and Tom switched of the engine. He leant forward and rested his head on the steering wheel. Ava waited until he turned to her.

"Yes baby. We will be ok. Now let's get this over with"

They were hurtling along the dual carriage way, Sarah had turned her face away to hide the tears.

"You ok?" Ariel asked from the driver's seat. Sarah couldn't have drove, she could barely stand, so Ariel had taken the keys.

"No" she mumbled.

"I'm so sorry" Ariel offered.

"I loved him so much. I can remember that now. How can he be dead?"

"The report said he was knocked down"

Sarah slowly turned her face to Ariel "There was a report?"

"I just glanced over it, but I didn't think you would want to see" she offered in her defence. Sarah blinked at her.

"It was an accident Sarah, a freak accident"

Sarah's chest tightened. Hadn't she been in an accident too, wasn't this the reason all this was happening, all this confusion. John had claimed her. Even though she had left him, he had claimed her when she was vulnerable in the hospital and he had wooed her, after everything. Her stomach turned. How could he?

"We will be there soon. Are you ready for this?" the question jolted Sarah back to the moving car, which wasn't helping the overwhelming desire to be sick. She forced the awful memory to the back of her mind. But there was a flash, of something else. Of John's wicked face bearing down on her but as quickly as it appeared it went.

"Ready for what?"

"The truth?" Ariel answered eyes firmly on the roads ahead.

"I need to help Gabrielle" was all Sarah could muster, not certain if she was, in fact, ready.

The turn appeared up ahead, Sarah's body stiffened, she recognised it immediately and it scared her.

"You ok?" Ariel sensed the shift in her.

"Stop please stop"

"What?" Ariel asked "Seriously?"

"Yes, I'm going to be sick"

She pulled up and killed off her engine. Macy was fast asleep with the babysitter and she needed the truth. She wasn't going to live like this, like Rita had. No, she wouldn't accept the advice of her mother in law to "Turn a blind eye dear and be a good wife and mother, that's all was required"

Giving birth to Macy a few months earlier had hurt like hell, it had been a trauma and the way she had felt since, well that's the problem, she hadn't felt anything. She almost couldn't blame him, but the words of John Snr rang through her thoughts

"We need a boy Sarah darling, so best get another one on the way soon"

It seems such an archaic thing to say. Like her perfect little daughter couldn't inherit the legacy, couldn't cope with running his empire. Well she would show this family just how strong women could be. She climbed out the car and used the pass she had made for her by Mabel to open the door. Everything was in darkness, only lit by the bright moon outside, allowing a soft silvery light to guide her safe passage. Sarah climbed the stairs, her heart pounding in her chest, at the Club was he? She thought to herself. Stepping into the corridor the office at the end burnt a slither of light along the floor. She walked slowly closer, suddenly unsure of herself. Did she want to know the truth? Sarah straightened her shoulder s and her resolve, as she pushed open the door and stepped into the light.

"Mabel?" she gasped. Her friend! "John?"

"Oh my god Sarah!" Mabel screamed covering herself as best she could with her discarded shirt.

"Mabel what the hell?" Sarah stood, her mouth fell open.

"I'm so sorry" Mabel pushed him out of her and jumped down off the desk, clambering to grab her clothes. She fled the room but before she did she stopped at Sarah's side, her eyes filled with tears "Please forgive me. He made me" and she ran into the blackness.

"John?" Sarah turned on him. He was still standing proud his cock hard.

"Yes?" he smirked.

"What is going on?"

"Well what does it look like?" he answered calmly resting back on the desk. Sarah fought back the tears. Her pulse drummed in her ears "This is nothing to do with you" he continued.

"What? Its everything to do with me, and Mabel is my friend" Sarah shrieked "Forget about it, go home to Macy and never mention it again. Everything will be ok"

"No!" she gasped.

"Well if you are staying" he sneered, his eyes twinkling, the corners of his mouth turning up into a little smirk as he nodded down to his erection.

"Oh my god" she faltered "Wait, what did Mabel mean you made her?"

He lunged at her, fury cursing instantly through his veins, he pinned her against the wall my her throat.

"John" she protested but his grip took the sound from her.

"Who are you to question me?" he snarled. She had never witnessed this side of him, what had she married into. Her body began to tremble.

"You will keep your mouth shut and get on with being a wife and a mother" She shook her head, his grip was tightening, she couldn't breathe and could feel the blood congregating in her head.

"John" she tried "Stop!" She was becoming light headed and as the black spots began to appear before her eyes he released her, sending her crashing to the floor. That's when the first hit came as he kicked her hard in her stomach. She was dizzy. Her vision blurred. The anger at her catching him flowed down into his clenched fists, he kicked her again. When she tried to protest he slapped her hard with the back of his hand. Grabbing her wrists he slammed them down firmly above her head and still partially naked he climbed on top of her. Sarah's heart began to pound in her chest and her eyes flew open at the realisation of his intentions she shook her head, the sting radiating from her jaw. He punch her in her hard in her face, the pain was instant and overwhelming, but no sooner had it seared through her he grabbed the front of her hair and smashed the back of her head against the floor. She screamed with the blow but still she fought against him.

"Sarah you're pissing me off. You just need to pay for this mistake and then we can get on with our lives, don't make me keep hurting you"

He pushed open her trembling legs and, still pinning her down, he tore at her underwear with one hand.

She couldn't seem to move. Paralyzed with fear. He was a stranger to her. Tears pricked in her eyes.

"John please...I don't want to"

"Shut up" he snapped covering her mouth with his hand. He pushed down hard on her face, it hurt her, he could see the tears running down her reddened cheeks but that only made the pull of his erection harder.

She closed her eyes and cried, the vulnerability of her fuelled his thirst. This was his pleasure now, and as he rammed himself inside her the swell of his cock increased, he has missed the sensation of taking someone against their will. He drove himself in and out. He grunted. This was like a drug to him, to use someone for pleasure, he ripped open her top, having to stop and concentrate so he wouldn't release, he planned to enjoy her for a while, she had after all interrupted his previous encounter. This time, this one, he was going to drag out her ordeal for as long as he could.

"Sarah?" Ariel shouted.

"What?" she blinked away the terrifying memory, now she longed to forget again. She pined for her comforting innocence. How could this be true, and how had she lived with it? With herself?

"You were miles away, and you look awful, the entire colour has drained from your face"

"I just remembered something"

"Something good?" Ariel encouraged.

"No Ariel, something terrible. Something that happened to me, and I'm not sure how many times I had to endure it, but something that eventually lead to all this"

"What?"

"I knew he did it, the memory. But I didn't know this"

"Knew what Sarah?"

"That he raped me more than once" she whispered.

Chapter 21

Macy made no sound as she carefully placed each footstep on the black iron fire escape. Her brother followed quietly in her wake, watching with intent where she placed each of her feet as best he could in the darkness.

"Just here" Macy whispered as the approached the wooden door on the third floor. It seemed like they were quite high up and Eric was glad that he couldn't see exactly how far down it was in the darkness.

"This lock as always been dodgy, if you twist it a certain way" she strained. The door made a few banging noises as she fought with the lock.

"Mace shhhhhh" Eric warned.

"Hang on" she whispered back until there was a click and the door limply slid open.

"See" she smiled back at him "Come on"

There was less light it here, it made walking the uneven surface of the abandoned mill more difficult "If we get to the open staircase at the end over there" she pointed dead ahead "We should be able to see a light source"

"Mace, I'm not sure about this" Eric grumbled uncertainly.

"Eric its fine, it's just dad and grandad"

"Yea, and look what grandad did to you!" he exclaimed.

"Forget about that he was just mad". A drop of liquid blobbed onto Macy's hair, and then another "Ew Shit" she squealed.

"What? What is it?!" Eric shot closer to her, the grey emptiness consuming him, prodding a sleeping terror he was trying to control.

"It's just a leak, but it landed right in my hair" She held on to him, almost dragging him to the stairwell. Macy looked up. Nothing. She peered down and there she could faintly make out a yellowish hue.

"Macy..."

"Shhhhhh" she silenced him and listened intently. There in the distance she could just about make out voices.

"This way!"

John paced up and down, occasionally stopping to look intently at Gabrielle sitting feebly on the couch. Edward had taken the seat next to her, mostly to calm her down. John snr had stormed off and was in thick conversation with the two men in the far corner of the vast cold room.

"This is how things will go" John started as he stopped in front of her "You can go home safe and sound, if you promise to leave Sarah alone. Just walk away"

"What?" Gabrielle looked up at him "Forget everything and leave her with you?" she spat.

"Gabrielle" John growled "Don't make this hard for yourself"

"What about Tom? You think you can just get away with that?"

Johns arm screamed with pain, as the blood pumped harder around his body, he could hear the thudding in his ears.

"Gabrielle, I feel it would be best to just walk away from this. I will make you a rich woman. Let me go home to Sarah and my children"

Gabrielle laughed chillingly. In an instant it had extinguished any compassion John had left for the woman he had been intimate with, striding to the desk he pulled open the drawer, retrieved the gun and with an outstretched arm, he aimed at her. She screamed "No please" she begged.

He marched confidently over to her, the gun felt secure in his hand even if his body ached, he was an old pro at this. Soon she could feel the overwhelming cold of the steel pushing up beneath her chin.

"I'm going to fucking kill you Gabrielle. I worked too hard to get my family back, to get her back. If you ruin this well, I'm going to fucking kill you and make it look like an accident just like I did with Tom"

Everyone's eyes fell on him. Edward backed away but the expression of the three remaining spectators failed to change.

"Ok, I'll leave, I'll leave and never come back" she whimpered a tear running from her eye, her head that far back with the force the feeling was unnatural, and she worried he would push it completely from her neck.

"Do you promise, do you fucking promise?" he screamed at her, his breath hitting her face. She looked into his eyes that now flashing and dancing with fire, remembering a time they had done the same with desire.

"I promise" she cried.

"I will kill you" he lowered his voice, but not relinquishing any pressure on the gun "If I ever see you again, I will fucking kill you do you understand?"

Gabrielle nodded her head as best she could, her hands trembling in her lap.

"John" Edward ventured.

He hesitated momentarily, unsure of his next move. She had forced him to play this hand and his body raged with fury. Why couldn't she just play nice?

"So how much shall I make the cheque out for?" John Snr shouted over to her as his son laboured to his feet. "Will one million do it? Keep your pretty little mouth shut dear?"

Gabrielle nodded slowly, her throat had tightened at the release of the gun, when the surge of realisation ran through her, he had threatened to kill her, and worse still see believed him for he had done it before. Nausea consumed her again, she fought to hold down the meagre contents of her stomach. Somewhere high above them Macy fought back tears.

"Here we are" Ariel slipped the car into park and clicked on the assisted handbrake, she surveyed the imposing building towering over them. It appeared empty but both women knew it wasn't. "You ready?" she looked to Sarah who hadn't moved.

"No" she mouthed "But Gabrielle is in there and I need to help her"

"She's not alone either" Ariel nodded to the car parked down the side of the building mostly hidden from view. The moonlight fell softly on the back of the silver Mercedes.

"I hadn't even noticed that"

"Well lady, it's a good job I'm here" Ariel offered a small chuckle but Sarah failed to partake in the sport. Tom was dead and Gabrielle was locked up somewhere inside this dark building, and why? She feared it was all because of her.

"Wait here" Sarah demanded as she released herself from the seatbelt with a click.

"No way" Ariel grabbed a laptop from the back seat firing it into life and clambering out into the cool night air "Follow me"

She crept over to the corner, setting the laptop down she took out some wires, put them in her mouth and silently scaled the window.

"What are you doing?" Sarah whispered.

"I'm hijacking their cameras" she mumbled down, taking out a pen knife and with some scrambling and twisting, she jumped back down "Watch" she said sitting before the now illuminated screen. Sarah watched her fingers work fast until in no time at all they were staring at Gabrielle on a couch with a gun held to her chin.

"What the fuck?" Sarah gasped her hands flying to her mouth.

"Jesus, is that a gun?" Ariel looked up and Sarah nodded.

"I think so"

"Shit you gotta get in there"

"What am I supposed to do?"

"Help her!"

"How Ariel?"

"You don't think he will shoot her do you?"

Sarah took a moment, a few weeks back the answer would have been full of confidence, no of course not, but now, now she wasn't sure what this man, her husband, was capable of.

"I don't know"

"Why does he have her anyway?" Ariel blinked in the brightness, the horrifying image of Gabrielle behind her.

"I wish I knew"

Ariel turned back to the screen, she had an idea and began to flick through all the other camera angles.

"What are you doing?" Sarah asked.

"If I can find the power source I can kill the electricity and we can get her out of here"

"What, this isn't fucking Mission Impossible, we are not Tom Cruise! What if he shoots at us?"

"Any better ideas?" Ariel whispered back continuing on her quest "Shit"

"What?" Sarah looked down, her heart quickened and her stomach dropped as the image of Macy and Eric in the beams above them filled her watery eyes.

"I don't like this Tom" Ava held tight on to him as they walked across the dark desolate car park.

"Its fine, don't worry" he gave her hand a reassuring squeeze. The door opened as they approached and a familiar face bore down at her.

"Mabel?" Ava muttered "What are you doing here?"

"Come in Sarah. Everyone is waiting" Mabel's eyes fell onto the clear bulge of Sarah's' stomach and gasped. Sarah froze. Her legs refused to move, Tom tugged at her.

"Baby?"

"What do you mean everyone?" Sarah managed to croak ignoring the wide eyed gawp coming from the woman in front of her, who was she too judge. Sarah had witnessed Mabel's character for herself.

"Just come inside Sarah" she opened the door wider and gestured for them both to enter.

"Ava, Sarah I mean" Tom started, "Come on. I'm here with you, nothing will happen, you are safe"

She desperately searched his pleading green eyes. Looking between him and her old friend, now impatiently tapping her foot, a surge of anger shot up Sarah. With her shoulders back and her head high she began to put one foot in front of the other appearing much more confident than she felt inside as she passed Mabel. Mabel held eye contact firmly with her until she was forced to look away and lock the door behind them.

"Boardroom" was all Mabel said. Sarah instinctively turned left through the double doors and climbed up the stairs, her hand still protectively engulfed within Tom's.

"You ok baby?" he whispered.

"I just want to see my children" she added her gaze fixed up on the top floor where she knew her past was waiting but as she reached the last steps she needed to take a couple of deep breaths. Tom placed his hands on her shoulders.

"I'm here ok. We are in this together and we are not leaving here without access to Macy and Eric"

She nodded and pushed through the double doors, at once she felt an arm around her neck as she was dragged sideways.

"Whoa" Tom shouted his hands up.

The grip around her neck got tighter as she grabbed frantically at the arm, until the sight of the gun in the corner of her eye stopped her dead. It was pointing straight at Tom, where another slightly smaller, stocky guy dressed head to toe in black, a number of weapons around his legs, was digging his gun into Tom's back.

"I see you have been introduced. Roger, let's take her through, Dave take him out back" Mabel purred, pointing a long manicured fingered at a stunned Tom.
"What no wait" Sarah screamed.
"It's fine" Tom nodded eyes boring into Sarah *"I will be fine"*

"I know a way in" Sarah said as the memory slipped away from her "It will be how Macy got in"
Ariel grabbed the laptop and followed behind, ducking passed the side of the Mercedes. The two women, with the small light emerging from the laptop crept their way around the back and up the fire escape. The door was open. Sarah followed in what she knew were Macy and Eric's footstep's, confident she could get to where they needed to be undetected, after all it had worked for them.
"What's going on Mace?" Eric begged his sister, she turned to him glassy eyed.
"I don't know" she turned to stare at him.
"Dad, killed someone?" he gasped.
"Let's get out of here. Be careful" Macy instructed, getting back wasn't going to be as easy as getting out here had been. Eric shimmied back along the thick beam on which they had enjoyed a terrorising bird's eye view of the events unfolding far beneath them. As he got closer to the platform leading out into the stairwell his hand slipped, his body tilted to the right, he felt himself loose the grip of his legs as the momentum started to swing them out. He was falling and Macy was looking the other way. He tried to cock his arm around the beam to stop his fall but he missed and just as his eyesight faced down at the concrete metres below and he waited for the weight of his body to push him down, hurtling to the floor, there was a jolt.
"Argh" he yelped.
Macy's head shot round and she locked eyes with her mother.
"It's ok, I got you!" Sarah had thrown herself out, just managing to grab him underneath his arm pits, half her body on the platform, weighted down as Ariel held her legs.
"Ava?" Gabrielle yelled from below.
"What the fuck?" John Jnr looked up "Sarah? Macy? Eric?"
The two other men had instantly pulled out their weapons and pointed in the direction of Eric's scream.
"No put your guns down" John yelled watching helplessly as Sarah dragged Eric to safety.
"Bring them here" John Snr demanded.
Their footsteps echoed quickly around the concrete stairwell as the men ran up, its once green paint cracking and crumbling from the wall. Sarah was faced with a gun, again. The smaller man smirked at her.
"You" she breathed "You killed Tom!" she spat at him.
"No mum, Dad killed Tom" Eric added.
"Eric" Macy chastised as Sarah turned to gawp at her son.

"What? What did you say?"

"Come on, downstairs now" the two men gestured in the direction with their guns. They followed silently, Sarah unable to process Eric's revelation as behind them Ariel hid in the shadows.

He shoved her hard into the room. The first face she saw was her husbands, disapproval written all over it.

"Where is Tom?" Sarah demanded as Mabel slinked in and took a seat next to John behind the long table

"Tom's safe, for now" John muttered his chin resting on his hands, clasped together as if in prayer.

"What do you want?" Sarah demanded, glancing sideways she was staring down the barrel of a pistol. Mabel whispered something to him and his gaze fell on his wife's stomach. Her hands automatically sprang to protect it.

"Take a seat Mrs Ryan" John demanded.

"I'm fine standing"

John looked at the man to her right and he forced her down by digging the gun into the top of her shoulder, she couldn't stand against the pain and found herself in the chair.

"We need to talk. You are coming home" John's hazel eyes burned into hers, Sarah shook her head "You have nothing and no one without me"

"I have Tom"

"Oh really? Where is he then?" John sat back and opened up his arms to the room, "He not here is he Sarah?"

"Because you took him away at gun point!" she shrieked.

"Well, that's a good point" John chuckled.

"He won't be harmed though. On one condition"

"What?" Sarah snapped.

"Well you see, I'm not a man you leave Sarah. I'm not a man whose wife walks out on him. I am John Ryan for god sake" he slammed his fist on the table

"And I have made enough excuses for you for the past six months. Enough is enough. You come home and Tom is released, all safe and sound"

"If I don't?"

John shrugged "Who knows?"

Sarah's heart drummed, would he really do this?

"I fucking promise you this Sarah, tonight you are coming home, it's up to you if Tom gets home or not"

"You wouldn't" she breathed the tears stinging at her eyes.

"I won't have you walk out on me, you are my wife, and you will be a wife and stay at home where you are supposed to be" he boomed. Sarah was unsure if it was the volume or the way he sneered that caused the trembling of her body.

"Sarah" Mabel started "Do the right thing, forget about Tom, and come home. At least for Eric and Macy"

"You won't ever see them again Sarah. If you try to escape again. If you try to leave me, I will keep them from you forever. You can't fight me, I have money Sarah, you can do anything when you have enough money"

Her mouth went dry as the tears streamed down her cheeks "How can you do this to me, when you know" she stared straight at Mabel, and for a second the smugness fell from her face, but she recovered quickly.

"It's best for everyone" Mabel answered.

Sarah hung her head. She knew this day was coming, she knew she couldn't defeat the mighty Ryan family and she knew what she was subjecting herself too. She felt sick. There was never going to be a choice. He would always own her.

"I'm pregnant"

"Well it can't exactly pass it for mine, so that's where Mabel comes in. She's going to adopt the baby and raise it as her own, at least then you can see it"

"What?! No!"

"It's the only way, and I have always wanted to be a mother Sarah, you know I will take care of it, and when John allows you can visit" Mabel offered.

"Please John" she sobbed "Don't do this, let me be happy"

"It's done" John stated "Now get up we are going home"

Sarah sat. Her palms in her lap, her head down. She didn't move until he grabbed her forcefully under her arm and dragged her up.

"Come on. Up" he demanded.

Her legs didn't want to work.

"You will stay at Mabel's until the baby is born and then you will be allowed home to see our children. Don't worry though, meet your babysitter" John smiled at the man holding the gun "Now let's go and we will release Tom, with terms of course"

John manhandled her down the corridor, retrieving the keys from his pocket with the free hand. She held her stomach as her heart ached.

"Go tell him" he directed Mabel "Meet us outside".

She sauntered off but moments later there was a loud bang in the distance. Sarah jumped. Her heart rammed into her throat. John looked at the man holding the gun. Then there was another. Sarah screamed.

"Go!" John demanded as he dragged her faster down the stairs towards the door

"Tom" she screamed fighting, trying to get free.

"Sarah!" John warned "Stop fighting me"

"Let me go!" she sobbed and in a moment of opportunity as his grip loosened Sarah kicked him as hard as she could between his legs, as John curled up and fell to the floor groaning she grabbed the keys that had slipped from his hand. She ran down the corridor, John rolling around in agony behind her

"Sarah" he growled as he watched her silhouette burst out of the door and into the night.

"Kids!" John yelled and ran to them as the three of them enter the vast room. Eric and Macy flinched from his embrace. Sarah felt the cold prod of the pistol in her back and edged forward.

"Edward take the children home now" John demanded "Hey kids everything will be ok" he knelt to speak to Eric "Mum and I will be home soon and I will explain everything, it's not what you think ok"

"Did you kill someone?" Eric pleaded, his eyes filling with water.

"No son. I promise. Trust me. I will explain"

Macy looked at her mother "Mum?"

"Go honey, everything will be ok" Sarah nodded as both her children were gently lead from the room as Edward took one last long look at Sarah.

"What are you doing here?" John turned on her.

"I remember" she answered a small tear releasing from the corner of her eye.

"Sarah" John started.

"Ava" Gabrielle whispered as Sarah acknowledged her "I didn't know he was your husband I promise" Sarah's brow furrowed as she turned to John, a smile blossoming on her face.

"Ah, I see. You're John England. Very original"

"How else did I get to find you, to keep you safe?"

"Keep me safe!" Sarah shouted "You spied on me!"

"You left! You went to Malta and you never came home and I thought you were dead!" John shouted "But then! Then I realised my wife had finally run off with him, with Tom! Who you promised you would finish it with"

"What?!" Sarah shook her head in confusion, a flash of an argument ran through her brain, John throwing her phone, it smashing to pieces on the hard tiled floor of their kitchen.

"Ah you don't remember everything then? You don't remember you were sleeping with him for a long time before I found out. You promised, for Eric and Macy"

"You were sleeping with Mabel! I saw her text, to leave me and she would forgive you!"

John let out a laugh "I'm not sleeping with Mabel, once, I did once, a long time ago, drunk and she wanted more, but I only wanted you. She wanted me to leave because of what you put me through over the last six months. We had an argument, I fired her because she kept hounding me and threatening to tell you everything. Then everything would have been for nothing. We may have fought a lot before, argued, screamed but that's all Sarah."

"I couldn't stay!"

"Why? Why Sarah?" John pleaded his fist clenched tightly beside him.

"You know why!" Gabrielle interrupted jumping to stand at her friend's side "You raped her"

Since this exchanged had started John Snr had stepped back, looking to slip out undetected.

"So you keep saying Gabrielle, is that what she told you?"

"Yes?" Gabrielle looked uncertainly at Sarah "He raped you, you told us, Tom and I. That's why you left?"

Sarah shook her head "No"

John folded his arms in triumph.

"Not him. Him" and she pointed at the old man trying to escape.

Chapter 22

"Dad?"

John Snr old body spun slowly, his eyes looking up and meeting his sons. He shrugged with a smile. "Son I do what I want, you know that"

"She's my wife!" John Jnr growled "The mother of your grandchildren"

"She's a slut that was cheating on you"

"Was I cheating on him when I found you with Mabel?"

"Mabel?" John Jnr gasped

"Ah she was more consenting, not a much fun as you Sarah, not as much fight. So what? Everything has worked out. Sarah is home, wives don't leave Ryan men. You want to count yourself lucky you didn't get the beating Rita did. First and last time she tried to leave"

"Everything has worked out? Tom is dead and so are my babies"

"Well that's not my fault" John Snr grinned menacingly.

"No it's his fault" Gabrielle pointed at John Jnr.

"His?" John Snr laughed "Oh ladies please" he strode confidently into the room "It's not his fault Tom is dead, it's hers you stupid girl" and he pointed straight at Sarah.

"What?" Sarah whispered, her stomach dropping like she had just been punched

"That's right, isn't it son. You killed Tom Sarah, all this fucking time, all this fucking effort has been because of my soft son's need to protect you, you undeserved slut"

"Father!" John warned

"What?" Sarah whispered again bending over to try to catch her breath, holding herself up by the knees.

"Oh you remember what I did, but not what you did princess? You are not innocent. You are a murderer and we are your only protectors"

The car bleeped open as she scrambled inside and locked it quickly. He may be behind her, she needed to run. To grab Eric and Macy and run. She fumbled with the keys, her hands shaking she dropped them.

"Shit"

As she sat upright she jumped at the slight of his face at the window. He banged it with his fist.

"Sarah!" John yelled.

She managed to jam to key into the ignition and the car roared to life.

"Sarah. Please. Stop" He yelled through the glass.

She slipped it into first gear and drove away John spinning off the body. The was a shot at the car, a huge ping and she heard in the distance John shouting for him to stop firing, Sarah had ducked down, but as she looked back up she

saw Tom running out in front of her. Her foot slammed on the brake as his eyes, wild with shock met hers and everything went black.

"I killed him" Sarah whispered.

"What?" Gabrielle bent down to help her up.

"I remember. I hit him with the car, the accident. That's what it was"

"Well, well, well, someone's finally caught up" John Snr declared his arms outstretched.

"Sarah its ok, I took care of it. I made it look like an accident" John took a step closer to her but she held up her hand.

"What about my babies?" she demanded, suffering tearing through her.

"You didn't have a seat belt on" John muttered "You hit Tom and then a wall and went through the windscreen. Edward couldn't save the babies"

She let out a cry. Her knees buckled beneath her, John dashed over in time to catch her and gently placed her on the couch. She had killed Tom and she had killed her children.

"All this drama" John Snr huffed "That's why we made you forget"

"What?" Sarah sobbed into her hands.

"I asked Edward to drug you so you wouldn't remember. So you could come back to your old life and we could be happy. I did all this for you" John Jnr admitted as he knelt before her.

"For me? You drugged me!" she cried

"Stop whining, you are safe aren't you? There has been no repercussions from your little murdering spree has there!" but before the final syllable could be uttered by John Snr he felt the full force of his son's fist against the side of his face. There was an almighty crack and the old man fell to his knees. The blood filled his mouth as it turned up into a smile.

"About time you grew some balls son" he whispered spitting blood on the floor

"I don't ever want to see you again, do you understand?"

John Snr laboured upright and faced his son.

"You don't have any choice boy, just like her" he nodded to where Sarah stood her hands over her mouth "You cannot escape either"

John clenched his fists again.

"I will give you time to digest, but the Launch is in three days, I will see you in the boardroom, if you want to inherit the business that is?" he wiped at his mouth with the sleeve of his jumper, never taking his eyes from his son.

"Just get out" John Jnr shouted "Everyone out!"

"Fine by me. Sarah" John Snr smiled at his daughter in Law, the glint of his eye inducing nausea within her.

"Gabrielle" John shouted as the two men lead her after the confident strides of John Snr "we have a deal remember?" he warned.

She nodded, a million pound richer "Ava, sorry Sarah. Can I call you?" She asked over her shoulder. Sarah looked at John, he nodded. Then they were alone. Sarah was exhausted, she couldn't stop the tears. John punched a message in his phone.

"Edward is back to take us home, to our children. Where you belong" he urged Sarah.

"I need to go to the toilet" she mumbled.

"Over there" John pointed, slumping back on the couch.

"I won't be long"

"Good and then we can put all this behind us and you can go back to being my wife"

"And your father?" Sarah asked

"We won't see much of him" John looked away his eyes burning.

The cold water on her face helped extinguish the tears. She gazed up at the mirror, her stare returned by a woman she didn't recognise. Huge red eyes. She heaved again, but now only yellowish liquid was coming up. She had killed them all, Tom and their babies, and she didn't know how she was ever going to live with herself.

"Sarah"

She jumped.

"Ariel"

"I'm so sorry" Ariel offered "That's some mad shit right there"

Sarah nodded feebly.

"Listen I have something for you" she slipped a pen drive into her hand "I had a good view from up there, and a camera. If ever you feel in danger. Use this. It shows John's dad admitting to everything"

"What? But..."

"Don't ask questions. Not even the greatest computer whizz will ever know it's been, well slightly doctored. Take a look when you can. I have emailed it John Snr, untraceable of course, and I have told him if he ever comes near you again I will release it to the press and that will be their empire down the drain and him in prison"

"Ariel!" Sarah began to cry.

"No! No tears. Now go home. Live with the children you have, the one's you lost are safe with their father"

"I don't think I can"

"Yes" she lifted Sarah's chin so their eyes met "You can"

Ariel slipped out of the window with one last smile and into the night.

Chapter 23

The sun shone high in the cloudless sky, perfect. Straightening up the entire cutlery on the long outdoors table she smoothed down the tartan tablecloth. Bunting hung from the lush branches above her and she flicked on the round bulbed fairy lights that draped the branches. They weren't needed now but she knew her husband would expect everything to run smoothly. Caterers were busy in her kitchen, releasing a heady mix of garlic and spices into the air. She took a moment to breathe it in and gazed out along the large manicured lawn to the lake beyond. Her chest expanded and released, her hands resting on her hips. They would be here soon, her guests and so she must get changed into the dress laid out on their bed upstairs. It had taken John a while to choose from her wardrobe last night, but she would dutifully wear anything.

"Sarah come on, John will be home soon" Adele shouted from the upper patio.
"Oh yes sorry" she smiled at her and rushing inside she was greeted by Maria and Vinny.
"My darling, what can we do to help?"
"Maria, nothing at all. The caterers have everything under control. This party is for you to enjoy. No working!" Sarah laughed.
"She can't help it my dear, idle hands and the Devil she says, or something" Vinny smiled at his wife.
"I want to be of use Mela. My mind is so excited to see her. Your first Grandchild is very special"
"I can't remember…" muttered Vinny as he took the glass of whiskey he had sneakily ordered from a waiter.
"Ah, ignore him!" Maria said "It's very special"
"I know, I just want them home" Sarah answered "but first I must get changed. Please sit outside, get a drink, I won't be long" and she kissed Maria's cheek and took the stairs two at a time.
"Edward isn't far, he got Macy and Eric from the station no problem, he says she's beautiful" Adele was standing in Sarah's bedroom adjusting her earring in the mirror.
"What time do Aaron and Dennis arrive back from University?"
"They will be here after five" Adele had missed her sons, the house felt so much bigger without them there.
"Great. I will just quickly change."
"Ok, oh and John text to make sure you remember to wear the new sapphire necklace his parents bought you for your birthday"
"Oh course" Sarah's throat tightened a little, but as usual she smiled it away "I wouldn't forget that, it's beautiful"

Sarah stood before the mirror, the velvet black dress clinging to her curves, the cut of the neck a little too low for her liking, pushing more of her breast out than she cared to show but John had picked it and she want to please him. She opened the box on the dresser before her, the diamonds dancing in the light, as if announcing the large blue stone they held in the middle. She lifted it carefully, swallowing hard, and placed it around her bare neck. It clicked into place, she dropped her arms to take in the effect. It strangled her.

"Wow!" John whistled as he entered her dressing room "quick before my wife gets home" smiling he slid a hand over her bottom and around her waist pulling her in to kiss.

"Welcome home darling" she said.

"You look beautiful" he smiled down at her and relished the blush she had perfected over the years.

"Thank you"

"The necklace is nice"

She stroked it "Yes, such a thoughtful gift, they know I love sapphires"

"Yes they do" he kissed her nose, brushing away any thoughts of the past as they always did. He slid a strap down over her shoulder

"I enjoy how this dress is pressing against your tits" he grinned as he caressed her chest with his strong hand. She smiled, understanding the lust in her husband's eyes.

"Maybe we have time quickly?" he murmured "Turn around" he whispered.

Sarah did as she was told, he hitched up the dress and kicked open her legs He pulled down the tight fabric, her breasts bouncing into freedom. Once his trousers were unbuckled he yanked her knickers to one side, grabbed both her breasts and penetrated her. Sarah knew the noises to make. She knew when he liked silence and when he liked performance. Today she held her tongue as she closed her eyes, waiting for her husband to finish with her. It didn't take long before he shuddered and came inside her. Pulling out he walked away.

"I need to nip into the shower, make sure you are down to greet everyone, after all it's not very often we get to introduce everyone to our first grandchild" he said and she nodded while she readjusted her dress.

"Oh and tie up your hair it will look better with your outfit darling" he added. Dutifully she grabbed some pins and folded he hair into a pleat.

"Mum!" Macy came bursting through the large door of their manor house. Sarah ran too her, engulfing her into a warm embrace.

"Hi Mum" Eric wrapped himself around both women without disturbing their greeting. He towered over them both now, clearly getting the height from his father but still his features resembled Sarah's.

"Hi Sarah" Michael, Macy's husband entered behind carrying the car seat

"Oh let me see her" Sarah bent down to peer at her sleeping granddaughter

"She's been asleep the whole journey" Macy laughed "Get her out Mike, she could do with a feed and mum can have a cuddle"

"No wait, let her sleep. I need to check everything is ok before your father gets down and then I will come and steal her"

"Mum?" Macy moaned.

"Its fine honey, you know he likes everything perfect. Hi Edward" They embraced

"Hello Sarah, you look beautiful as ever" the phone in his hand vibrated and Sarah noticed the caller.

"Clara?" Sarah whispered, stunned.

"She called me a few weeks back out of the blue, please believe me Sarah. She is selling the flat to move in with her husband. She needed some paperwork. I promise that's it, please don't mention anything to Adele" he pleaded. He had kept her secret for all these years hadn't he?

"Ok, ok. Adele's in the garden come with me" she smiled and lead him outside for a final check.

"Get the monster out then, I will feed her" Eric chuckled as the all sat in the kitchen

"Where's my granddaughter" John beamed as he entered the room

"Hi dad" Macy kissed him,

"John" Mike shook his hand and offered him the car seat, where she still slept soundly.

"Wow! Mum's done a great job" Macy whistled seeing the pink themed back lawn.

"Yes, she's super at these things" John cooed at the now waking baby.

"Macy, Anna is awake can I grab her" Eric asked

"Sure, I will heat a bottle"

"How's business Mike?" John asked sitting at the large square table and ushering him into a seat. John had met Mike all those years ago in Manchester when he had done a deal to purchase their rival sports brand, led by Mike's father. He showed promise and not long after, he had paid for the Tuscan wedding to his only daughter. He was already seeing returns from Mike's information and decisions which had expanded John's brand. He recently promoted him to Head of Investments

"Great, great. Looking at a new office in Hong Kong"

"Excellent"

"Oh boys, no work today, it's about Anna" Macy smiled passing the bottle to her brother and kissing her smiling daughter. The doorbell chimed and one of the hired staff disappeared to greet the steady stream of guests.

Rita and John arrived being shown into the kitchen as Sarah re-entered to request top ups on champagne outside.

"Sarah darling!" Rita sang rushing over in a symphony of clanging jewellery.

"Hello Rita" Sarah air kissed her mother in law "John, welcome" she smiled at both his parents, rubbing down her skirt and patting at her hair.
"Where is she?" Rita chimed "Where's my great grandbaby?"
"Here Grandma" Eric shouted from the couch at the end of the family room where he was quietly rocking his niece
"Lovely job with the decoration's Sarah" John Snr noted.
"Thank you" Sarah said slipping into the held out arm of her husband "Shall we all head outside get a drink?" she smiled.
"Yes, good idea" John Snr agreed.

Sometime later, when everyone had been seated and served their afternoon tea. When the champagne and the vodka's had been topped up. When the quartet had completed their set and the warmth of the day has subsided, the light shifted. Sarah took a moment to escape with baby Anna safe in her arms. She slipped off the excruciating court shoes John liked her to wear and took a step onto the lush cool grass. She carried her granddaughter down the lawn, past the topiary and the rose bushes, the sweetness following long after. She crossed the small bridge over the glistening lake and sat quietly on the stone bench. The birds were tweeting, getting ready to settle in for the night and she could just hear the soft music from the lightly illuminated large house behind her, if she strained. She breathed the fresh sticky air and looked down at that cherub face, her soft eyelashes resting on her plump cheeks. Sarah's heart swelled. Anna wrapped a podgy hand around her grandmother's finger, and Sarah wished she could make her understand that she was wrapped around her heart. Forever. She felt him take a seat beside her.
"She's beautiful you must be very proud"
"You took my babies. How could you do that to me Edward?" she spoke quietly, the words that had burned in her chest for almost five years.
"I'm so sorry Sarah, I really am" tears sprang in his eyes as he leaned back and sighed.
"What were they?"
"A boy and a girl" Edward answered quietly, looking down to his intertwined fingers resting in his lap, his heart aching for this shadow of a woman next to him.
"Tom would have loved that" she turned her face up to the fading sun, feeling the sleeping baby breathing heavily in her arms. Edwards's heart raced and he shifted in his seat.
"I'm sorry Sarah, I meant to tell you this a long time ago but after everything...Well I just couldn't find the words"
She froze, turning slowly to face him "What? What is it?" she blinked.
"The babies, they weren't Toms. They were Caucasian"
Sarah gasped, shaking her head "What? No!"
"I'm so sorry Sarah" he offered

"No!" she muttered

"Maybe John will want to know, it may change things? Maybe he won't be as demanding of you"

A lone tear fell down Sarah's cheek and she stifled a sob.

"Oh Sarah" Edward put his arm around her in comfort "I shouldn't have said anything"

They sat in silence for some time, just them, the small sleeping baby and the birds in the trees. Eventually the tears stopped.

"Thank you. For telling me. It helps"

"It helps?"

Sarah rose, got a secure but gentle grip on Anna.

"Yes, I may have killed the man I love, but at least now I didn't kill his babies. Only the children of my Father in Law" and she wandered back towards the lit up house where the party continued.

Acknowledgments

So they say everyone has a book in them. In fact "they" have mentioned this an awful lot since the publication of my first novel Alluvia. I wrestled with this thought throughout the writing of Lost Woman Within, but I am pleased to say here I am, writing my Acknowledgments, the cluster of words resting comfortably behind me. What a pleasure it has been.

Firstly, and as always, I would like to thank my husband Matthew, whose interest in my stories hasn't grown since the last book, where it was already none existent. He's a doer, not a reader! But who's love, patience and uncomplicated views of the world has moulded my confidence, and allowed me the luxury of time, spent typing away. You are indeed my hero and sometimes unwilling, partner in crime. I am blessed.

Secondly to my children, for whom everything is ever done. I hope to inspire you to follow whatever dreams you hold most dear, and I promise to stand behind you in all of them, as the violent shove, if necessary. You inspire me each day. You also make me laugh like no one ever has, most of it inappropriate for print.

Again my parents and family, my friends who have been dragged along into these worlds of my creation, but have supported me anyway! There are so many to mention – Lucky me! You know who you are. Sarah, I hope the ending is now satisfactory. Kathryn, this one is definitely ripe for a film. Laura, I did it again! Kimberley, The Apprentice is going to have to wait. Lizzy, thanks for proof reading in the back garden on a sunny afternoon.

To Mrs Doyle, who got me out in front of the school year at fifteen to measure my skirt – it was 28cm too short, I guess it didn't matter after all!

Finally, to all those that got behind me to spread the news of my work. I appreciate it more than I can ever put into words, which shouldn't be true of a writer. Readers, new friends, helpers – you amaze me. Thank you. I feel like I am a community rather than just one. Awesome.

Stay Classy San Diego.

You can contact Jh Lewis on the following:
Facebook: www.facebook.com/jhlewisauthor/

Instagram: www.instagram.com/jh.lewisauthor/
Twitter: www.twitter.com/jenhlewi/

Download JH Lewis debut novel Alluvia on Amzon, Kindle and iBooks now.

8338382R00082

Printed in Germany
by Amazon Distribution
GmbH, Leipzig